A Sleigh Ride for

Aven

J. L. Dawson

A Sleigh Ride for Aven

By J L Dawson

Butterfly Books

PUBLISHING

Publisher's Note: This book is a work of fiction. Names, characters, places and incidents are products of the author's imagination or used in a fictional context. All characters are fictional, and any similarity to people living or dead is purely coincidental.

Cover design by: Nancy Fraser
Edited by: Evelyn Foreman & Sharon Dean

ISBN (Paperback) 978-1-7386018-6-8
ISBN (E-book) 978-1-7386018-5-1

A CiP catalogue record for this title is available from the National Library of New Zealand.

First edition, 2024 Butterfly Books Publishing

Contact the author or subscribe to newsletter:
jldawsonauthor@yahoo.com
www.jodawsonauthor.com

Contents

One

"No peeking, Papa." Eight-year-old Amelia gripped her father's hand tightly as she led him to the main room of their small cabin.

"Keep your eyes closed," Ada insisted. The pretty thirteen-year-old gripped her father's other hand.

"They are closed. What are you two up to?"

"It's a secret, Papa. Sit here." Amelia pulled a chair out for him.

Keeping his eyes tightly closed, Walter Miller gripped the chair and sat down. The aroma of candle wax and burnt pancakes filled his nostrils. He smiled. "May I look now?"

"Hold on, one more thing." Aven's voice came from the kitchen.

Walter heard his oldest daughter hurry toward the table as she placed something before him with a thud. Then the smell of hot coffee tantalized him.

"What is all this?" His eyes remained tightly closed.

"Okay, open your eyes, Papa." Amelia stood next to him.

Walter opened his eyes and looked around. A wide smile crossed his face. The usual breakfast of pancakes and bacon lay before him, the plates and silverware carefully positioned on the blue gingham tablecloth. His eyes fell on the unusual item, a pound cake with a candle poked into it. He grinned and looked from beaming face to beaming face. "What's this all about?" He turned to look at Aven.

"We wanted to do something nice for your birthday, Papa." She leaned down and kissed his cheek.

"Oh, is it my birthday?" His tone and sparkling eyes told them he was teasing.

"Of course it is, Papa." Amelia giggled.

"Oh yes, I suppose you're right, Poppet." He put his arm around her. "Thank you, my darlings. Pound cake is my favorite."

"We know, that's why we made it!" Ada plonked down on the chair next to his.

"You made it?" Walter's brows flew up.

"Well, Aven made it, but we helped."

Aven smiled at her sisters. "They did, Papa."

"Well, thank you, darling. We don't usually have cake for breakfast."

"It's your birthday, you can have a small slice." Amelia smiled.

"Blow out the candle," Ada prompted.

"Alright." Walter blew out the candle.

Amelia wrapped her arms around his neck and leaned her head on his shoulder. "Make a wish."

Walter lifted the eight-year-old onto his lap, kissed her hair and turned his eyes on his older two daughters. "I don't need to make a wish. I have everything I want already."

"Except Mama." Amelia's lip trembled.

Walter tightened his arms around her and his eyes flicked to the faded wedding photo hanging on the wall. He closed his eyes briefly and Amelia felt him shudder. "I know, darling. I'm sorry about ya Mama." This was his first birthday since his beloved Carolina had died the previous winter. "I'm so glad I have you girls." He reached up and cupped Aven's chin. "You are so much like her."

"I miss her, Papa." Aven brushed away a tear.

Walter leaned over and kissed her cheek. "I know, I do too, every day."

"If only we'd had a doctor, she might've survived."

"Darling, we can't live with regrets or bitterness. We don't know why God took ya ma, but He did. All we can do is live to make her proud and do our best with what the Lord has given us." He looked around. Their three-room log cabin was sparsely decorated but it was warm and full of love.

"You're right, Papa. Mama would want us to be happy." Ada gave him a brave smile.

"And she'd want you to do your studies and be the best girls you can be."

Ada groaned. "Ohhh. I hate studying history."

"Ada, we don't hate." Aven scolded. "And study is important, you know that. Mama said just because we live in a tiny town and there's no school here it doesn't mean we need to be ignorant. You used to want to be a teacher like she was before we moved here."

"Well, I don't anymore. Too much facts to learn!" Ada pouted.

"Too many," Aven corrected.

Ada poked her tongue out at her older sister.

"Now girls, how about we enjoy this good breakfast." Walter smiled. Internally his thoughts were all jumbled. He missed his Carolina more than he cared to confess. He'd done all he could to keep his girls spirits up, to keep their family going. He was grateful he had a good job and Aven was almost eighteen and more than capable of caring for their home. The ladies of the village had helped where they could, but they had their own families to care for and few had spare money.

"Pray, Papa." Aven's voice penetrated his thoughts.

He smiled, reached out his two hands to grip Aven's and Ada's. They in turn took Amelia's hands and the family bowed their heads in prayer. The three girls repeated their father's 'Amen' and waited for him to stack three pancakes on his plate.

Aven placed one on her own plate and one on each of her sister's, then placed the larger dish down. Four more golden pancakes remained.

Walter swallowed a mouthful of pancake and looked up at Aven. "Are you going to town this morning?"

"We're running low on flour, salt and a few other staples, so I'll get to the store after I do the wash and and get the girls set up with their studies." Aven grimaced, mentally counting their money hoping the meagre amount would stretch.

"Can we come with you?" Ada spoke with her mouth full.

Aven scowled at her lack of manners. "No, I need to visit a few of the neighbors. I promised the Widow Bransen I'd trade some of Ma's preserves for a small ham."

"Mmmm. I love ham." Amelia licked her lips comically.

"I know, darling, that's why I'm doing it, it's been a while since we've had any." Aven squeezed her younger sister's arm. "It'll be a delicious treat."

"I'm so glad her son raises pigs." Ada grinned.

"Me too. They are most generous to all of us in the town. Pork makes a change from the usual beefsteak or elk." Aven screwed up her nose. She'd never really enjoyed the flavor of elk or some of the other game her father brought home. Still, she was grateful to have the meat, so she changed her grimace to a smile. "I'm thankful to God for the kindness of our neighbors."

"Me too." Walter smiled and wiped his mouth on his napkin. "Well, I'd best get to work."

"Wait, Papa! I'll wrap up some pound cake for you to take with your lunch." Aven stood up and stacked her plate on top of her father's.

"I'd like that, darling. I'll go hitch Bert to the gig and come back in for my pail."

"Of course." Aven hurried to the kitchen to pack up her father's lunch, while the two younger girls cleared up the table. Amelia whipped off the tablecloth and pulled the schoolbooks down off the shelf, along with their slates and paper tablets. She screwed up her nose and hurried to the kitchen to help with dishes. Anything to delay having to study history.

Walter popped his head in the door. Aven passed him his pail. "Have a good day, Papa."

"I will, darling." He kissed her cheek then leaned down to kiss the cheeks of his other two girls. "You girls be good and mind your sister."

"Yes, Papa," the two chimed in unison.

"Get your schoolwork done and make me proud. I never got much schooling and I want better for my girls. I want you to have more opportunities than I had, and that means you need to study." He gripped Amelia's chin and winked at her.

"Yes, Papa."

"That's my girl." He took the pail from Aven's hand. "See you for supper."

"See you then, Papa." Aven kissed his stubbly cheek. "We love you."

"I love you too, darling." Walter hurried out the door to the waiting gig.

Two

"Good day, Miss Miller." Mr. Jensen's thick Norwegian accent and deep booming voice rang out before she even got two steps inside.

"Good day, Mr. Jensen."

He smiled and tucked his pencil behind his ear. Rubbing his hands down his striped apron, he furrowed his brows as Aven approached him. "What ya need today?"

Aven passed him her list of the required pantry staples. He perused it and smiled, giving her a nod as she turned to look at the shelves.

"Soap," she whispered. Examining the small selection, Aven picked up a lilac scented bar and held it to her nose. Placing it down she picked up another and smelled it. One by one she brought each bar to her nose, letting the aromas tantalize her. How wonderful it would be to have the fragrant soaps for their baths. Holding a lavender bar to her nose, she closed her eyes and shook her head sadly, placing the bar back on the shelf.

Opting for the much cheaper lye soap, she added two large bars to her basket, and a wistful sigh escaped her lips. She hated the smell of the lye soaps, but they lasted a long time and could be used for the laundry as well.

"Practicality is more important than indulgence." She attempted to convince herself that fancy soaps were a frivolous expense. Still, she couldn't help but give the lilac soap one last sniff.

A rough hand slipped over Aven's as she placed the soap back on the shelf. The man stood very close to her and whispered in her ear. "I'll buy that for you, Aven."

Aven shuddered and snatched her hand back, stepping away from the man, hoping he couldn't see the revulsion she felt. "Ahhh... No thank you. Mr. Mitchell." *Be gracious, even to a person who is challenging to love.* Her mother's words echoed in her ears, but it wasn't what she wanted to do. Her first instinct whenever she saw Archie Mitchell was to run away. There was something about him that revolted her.

Archie was already thirty-five years old and very uncouth. He was the wealthy owner of the lumber mill her father worked for and had taken a liking to her since her family had arrived in Thief River Falls. The idea of a pretty young wife seemed intriguing to him, and he'd propositioned her on more than one occasion.

He smiled at her, making no attempt to hide his roving inspection of her figure. Aven lifted the basket to cover as much of herself as she could and stifled a shudder. Archie stood between her and the counter, trapping her by the back wall holding shelves of pots and pans and various household items.

"Don't be like that, Miss Aven. I wanna do ya a good turn is all. A sweet girl like you needs a sweet-smellin' soap." He leaned in and stroked her cheek, bringing his face close to hers and deliberately inhaling deeply. "Course ya already smell pretty."

Aven closed her eyes and stepped back from him, but there was nowhere to go except into the shelf. She took a deep breath and sucked back all the snarky remarks that swum in her mind. "If you don't mind, Mr. Mitchell, I'd like to make my purchases and go home; my sisters are waiting for me."

Archie ignored her and lifted a hand to her arm, gripping her tighter than she'd like. "I could give ya a good life, Miss Miller. A pretty young thing like you would make a fine little wife." He brushed her cheek.

Aven tilted her head away from him, the fear and loathing began to rise in her mind. Her skin crawled and his touch made her grimace visibly. There was no look of love or even desire in his eyes, just a calculating possessiveness that terrified her. She instinctively knew that a marriage to that man would be torturous. Thankfully before he could say anything more Mrs. Kelly strode around the corner. Archie released his grip on her and hurried away.

Aven shuddered and gave Mrs. Kelly a grateful smile. Hiding behind the shelf, she took deep breaths to calm herself and waited until Mr. Mitchell had left the store before making her way to the counter.

"Is dis all ya be needin'?" The kind storekeeper gestured to the small pile on the counter.

Aven nodded to the man and her eyes drifted above his head to the pretty little porcelain doll on the high shelf. Amelia's ninth birthday was coming up and she couldn't help thinking how much her sister would love that doll.

None of the girls had never had a store-bought doll. Amelia loved Mattie, the ragdoll their mother had made for Aven many years ago, but she was now threadbare in places.

I wish I could get that doll for her. She smiled and observed the doll's pale porcelain face and bright blue eyes and long brown curls tied up with blue bows. *She even looks like Amelia.* Aven's eyes drifted to the tag below. *Fifty cents.* She groaned internally, and pulled out her reticule. She'd be lucky to have four cents left over after this purchase. Her father had been unsuccessful at negotiating a pay raise for he and his crew.

They were not destitute, they had enough to get by and make their house payments if they were careful, but luxuries like fancy soaps and a new doll were far out of her reach and she knew it.

Aven turned her eyes back to the store man – still awaiting her answer. "Yes. Thank you, Mr. Jensen, this is all."

The man nodded and opened to a page in his large ledger that simply said 'Miller' at the top.

He ran his finger down the column of entries and grimaced. "Ya didn't pay for da last one."

"I know, I'm sorry, the payroll was stolen and Papa didn't get paid last month."

"Ya hafta pay." Mr. Jensen's eyes were full of sympathy, but he had a family to feed too.

Aven nodded. "How much all together?"

"One 'n' ten."

Aven closed her eyes. "One dollar and ten cents?" She raised her eyebrows and opened her reticule, pulled out a small handful of coins and put them on the counter. "I have..." She paused to count them, even though she knew full well it wasn't nearly enough. "Eighty..." She touched each penny as she counted, "nine cents." She grimaced, eyeing the pile to see what she could possibly return. It really was just the bare necessities.

Mr. Jensen picked up the coins one at a time. "Vhen ya gets da rest?"

"Papa gets paid on Friday. They've promised to cover the money they missed last month as well, so we can more than cover it." She sincerely hoped that was true. Ada had no pairs of stockings that didn't have mends in them and Amelia wore her older sister's worn old shoes, with newspaper stuffed in the toe and a piece of leather covering the hole, in a futile attempt to keep out water.

Both of her younger sisters desperately needed a new winter coat, and she couldn't let the hems of their Sunday dresses down anymore.

The man nodded and made a note in the ledger. "Friday. But ya 'afta pay."

"We will. I promise." She smiled as the man placed the groceries in her basket for her.

"Else, I put ya to vork." There was a slight twinkle in the man's eyes. He wasn't unkind but he was a businessman and had a wife and four children to care for.

"I understand." She smiled. "You've been most kind, Mr. Jensen." Aven picked up her basket and walked out into the sunshine.

Feeling eyes on her, she looked towards the saloon and stifled a shudder. Mr. Mitchell leaned against the high porch railing of the saloon; one arm resting on the rail. He lifted his cigarette to his mouth and smirked, leering at her. Exhaling a plume of smoke, he winked at her suggestively and ran his tongue across his top teeth.

Aven abruptly turned and hurried away, deliberately forcing her mind to concentrate on what she could do for Amelia's birthday with the little they had on hand. Perhaps she'd use the pretty candle her mother had been given and tie a hair ribbon around it. Aven shrugged. It seemed such a poor attempt at decorating the house for a celebration, but they couldn't afford to purchase anything.

"What can I give her for a gift?" Aven muttered under her breath. "If only I could afford that dolly."

She shook her head sadly and continued to speak her thoughts aloud as she walked. "The best I can do is gingerbread boys…" Her thoughts were brought to an abrupt halt by a loud rumbling. She gasped and turned her face in the direction of the sound as a large crash and splintering of wood echoed down the hillside in the direction of Circle Ridge.

A foreboding feeling washed over Aven. "Papa," she mumbled, dropped her basket and put both hands to her face, her eyes flooded with tears, and she let out a sob. Her father's crew was at Circle Ridge that day, a dangerous section of forest on the side of a steep hill.

Before the rumble had even finished, the boardwalks filled with townsfolk with wide eyes and worried faces, staring in the direction of Circle Ridge. No one spoke and all stood transfixed to their spots. The noise stopped and people looked to one another anxiously seeking an answer.

Harvey McCoy, a cowboy on his day off, leapt up from his spot outside the café and hurried to his horse, calling out as he ran, "Men, mount up, we'll ride out and make sure no one's hurt."

Several men nodded and hurried to follow. Those left standing around continued to stare as the men galloped out of town, flicking up dust from the road.

One by one the bystanders turned back to their business. It was likely nothing more than a tree rolling down and crashing into the ravine and it wouldn't be the first time. Mrs. McKenzie nodded to Aven. "Just a runaway log, nothin' ta worry 'bout, love." She smiled kindly and headed back into the mercantile.

But the foreboding feeling never left Aven. She closed her eyes. "Lord, please let Papa be alright." She drew strength from her prayer, scooped up her basket and strode toward her home.

Three

"Papa's awful late getting home." Amelia screwed up her nose and looked at the clock for the umpteenth time.

Aven placed a lid on the pot and wiped her brow with the back of her hand. She gave her sister a reassuring smile. "I know, darling, but he'll be here any moment, they'll just be marking the trees for tomorrow..." A loud knock on the door brought her sentence to a halt.

"Who could that be?" Ada frowned and put her book down, leaping up from the sofa to hurry to open the door.

Aven turned to stir the stew.

"Good day, Miss Miller."

Aven pivoted on her heels and looked up at the man in the doorway dressed in black from head to toe, apart from the small white collar. He wrang his hands together, the distraught look on his face and tremble to his lips made her inhale sharply. Next to him stood a slight woman, with delicate features and a shapely nose. She was simply dressed and carried a basket in her hands.

Aven hurried to the door. "Reverend, Mrs. Cartwright?" She couldn't ask the question, her pounding heart feared the answer.

"Might we come in?" The woman managed a caring, if somewhat shaky smile.

"Certainly. Ada, would you fetch the reverend and his wife some coffee please."

Ada sensed her older sister's tone and hastened to oblige.

"Please take a seat." Aven gestured to the table, struggling to hear her own words over the pounding in her ears.

The middle-aged pastor was a caring man, but he so hated to be the bearer of bad news. He looked to his wife, and she squeezed his hand gently, in unspoken support. He nodded his thanks and gratefully received the cup from Ada. He took a long and soothing drink and placed the cup on the table. Three sets of blue eyes examined his face in anticipation. Mrs. Cartwright nursed her cup and looked from face to face, concern and sympathy written all over her countenance.

Amelia stood next to Aven's chair and the older girl gripped the younger's hand supportively.

The reverend whispered under his breath in a barely audible voice, "Lord help me."

Mrs. Cartwright squeezed his arm again.

The man took a deep breath. "I'm sorry to come here like this, girls, but I'm afraid..." He paused, dreading the words to come. Glancing at his wife for courage he turned back to them. "I'm afraid there's been an accident."

Aven sucked in a breath and put an arm around each of her sisters. "Is it Papa?" Her voice trembled and she desperately fought the tears, attempting to remain stoic for her sisters' sake.

"I'm afraid so," the Reverend continued.

"Is he... Is he alright?" Ada bravely asked the question. "Is he hurt?"

Amelia turned her face to bury it in Aven's shoulder. She was already weeping. Aven squeezed her and stroked the girl's hair.

The pastor slowly looked from one face to the other. Mrs. Cartwright stood and walked around to place supportive arms around the girls.

"I'm afraid not." The man's voice was full of sympathy for the unfortunate situation the girls found themselves in. He decided the direct approach was probably best. Exhaling loudly he said quickly, "I'm afraid he was killed."

"Noooooo." The shrill agonizing cry of three voices hung heavy in the air and Mrs. Cartwright clung to them as they huddled together and sobbed.

"Papa," Amelia whimpered.

No one spoke for a time. The kind pastor walked around and squatted before Amelia to join the embrace. "I'm so sorry, girls, I'm so sorry." He sat back and looked at them.

Finally the three girls turned tear-filled eyes to him. "What happened?" Aven couldn't believe she was asking that question but a temporary peace washed over her, the comfort she knew only their gracious God could provide at such a time.

The reverend nodded and stood to take his seat again. He drained his coffee cup. "The short version is a pile of logs gave way and rolled down the hill, your father and eight other men were crushed. Five are dead, two seriously injured, and Mr. Smythe will likely lose his leg if he survives."

Aven's lip trembled and she nodded, registering the information slowly, still clinging to her distraught sisters.

"You should know, girls, that your pa was a brave and strong man. He rescued two men who were in the path of the logs, hauling them from the tree they were cutting and shoving them away before the logs reached them. He's a hero."

Aven nodded. "Yes." She managed a weak smile. Reality overcame her and her eyes flooded with tears again. "What are we supposed to do now, how will we make the house payments?"

Mrs. Cartwright gripped her shoulders. "God will be with ya. We'll help ya. Everyone in the town will help ya, however we can, but there's a lot of sadness in this town today."

"We'll stay here with you for a time, make sure you're all okay." The reverend smiled kindly. "If ya like."

"Thank you, Reverend. We'd appreciate that." Aven nodded.

*   *   *   *

Aven poured herself a cup of coffee and slumped into their threadbare armchair. She pulled a rug over her knees and put her cup down on the small table beside the chair. Leaning her head against the stuffed back of the chair, she lifted her eyes to the small cross hanging above the wedding photo on the mantle. She spoke her prayers aloud. "God, we're gonna need Your help." Her lips trembled and she swiped at the tears gathering in the corners of her eyes. "I don't know what we'll do to get by, but I know You're with us. Show me how to keep going, to look after my sisters and not lose our home. Help me keep us all together, please."

"He will."

Aven looked up in the direction of the voice. "Reverend?"

"I came out for a glass of water." He sat down in the chair opposite her. "I heard your prayer. You're a strong young woman, Miss Miller."

"I'm not so strong. I'm terrified if you must know. I don't know how to keep going, how to keep us together."

The reverend reached across and gripped her arm. "I'm really sorry, Aven. Life has dealt you all a pretty rough hand. It really doesn't seem fair sometimes, I know that only too well." He gave her a kind smile and squeezed her arm.

Aven nodded. She knew the story of how the faithful man of God had lost all three of his precious children. *Yes, he does know the pain of losing those ya love.*

The man continued. "But I also know you'll be alright, God is with you and even though it doesn't feel like it right now, He will see you through. He will help you if you lean on Him. And we'll help you too, Betty and Me. We don't have much to our names but whatever we can do to help we will."

Aven blinked back her tears and nodded. "Thank you. I appreciate that." But the reverend barely kept food on his own table at times. The people gave what they could to support him, but there were few in the small town who could be called affluent.

The reverend nodded and raised his brows. "You should get some sleep."

"I will. I just wanted to spend some time praying. Mama always said when life gets tough, no matter how tough, the first port of call is our God. He's got the biggest shoulders of all and will gladly help us bear our burdens."

"She was a wise woman." The reverend nodded. "And you're a lot like her."

"Thank you." Aven managed a shaky smile.

"Well, I'll leave you to it. Try to get some sleep, so you can be strong for your sisters."

"I know. I'm just glad they're sleeping."

He nodded to her. "Goodnight, Dear."

"Goodnight, Reverend."

Aven sat up until the small hours of the morning, petitioning God to help them, to keep them all together and to give her the strength to help her sisters have the wonderful life they deserved. "I will do anything to give them that, Lord."

Four

"Ashes to ashes, dust to dust..." The reverend's voice rang out across the cemetery to the somber crowd. Five fresh mounds of dirt lay before them. Mrs. Cartwright stood with her arms around Amelia and Ada and Aven stood beside them.

Sniffing away her tears she looked around at the scene. Four other families had lost their menfolk that day. Mrs. Thompson lost her husband and her eldest son. She stood in her black widow's garb and clung to her three younger children.

Aven gave the two littlest girls a kind smile. She turned her face to the other three women. Two with families and the last a young mother-to-be who'd only been married seven months. Aven let out a sob. There was so much sadness in the town.

The reverend concluded the short service and Aven noticed the man close his eyes and lower his head. A sob shook his body. He whispered something under his breath, squared his shoulders and stood up straight, determined to be the rock the town needed.

It was hard on a reverend, few knew how hard. With a town of broken and hurting people to help through a tragedy he'd need strength and support too. He turned his eyes to the heavens as the townsfolk somberly left the church yard. Aven paused to watch him, he lifted both hands up and nodded, as though drawing his strength from the Almighty.

Ada and Amelia walked with Mrs. Cartwright and the woman did all she could to comfort the two girls, she glanced back at her husband and murmured a prayer for him.

A movement caught Aven's eye and she smiled as a small robin flew down onto a low branch in a nearby tree and began his song. She paused to watch the little bird as it flicked its red tail and appeared to be dancing as it sang. Time seemed to stand still as she watched the little bird. There was something strangely healing in the scene, a happy bird letting her know the world would continue on as it always had, the sun would continue to rise and God had her in His hand.

She managed a wry smile and took a deep breath. "Lord, help us," she whispered.

Hearing feet swishing in the long grass behind her she spun on her heels and grimaced. Before she could walk away Mr. Mitchell gripped her arm tightly. He reeked of cigarette smoke and his breath was laced with alcohol. "I can help you." He gave her a smarmy smile.

Aven lifted frightened eyes to him. "Let me be."

Mr. Mitchell squeezed her arm. "I know ya ain't got any money and ya got the little ones to think of."

Aven could do little more than nod. He wasn't wrong.

"I can fix that."

Aven frowned. "How?"

He turned and spat on the grass and then eyed her up and down suggestively. "Come home with me. I got money, and a house."

Aven's frown increased. "What are you suggesting?" She didn't really want to know but she didn't know what else to do, save for pray. And pray she did, without ceasing.

He pulled her close to him, pinning her next to his body. Aven's eyes grew wide. "Leave me be." She tried to push away from him but he tightened his grip.

Before she could say anything else he leaned down and kissed her roughly. Aven let out a groan and tried to pull her head away. Archie gripped the back of her head tightly and continued the slobbery kiss. Aven squirmed and tried to get away from him, but he prolonged the kiss. Fear filled her mind. There was nothing romantic about that kiss, it was possessive and horrible.

He stopped the kiss but didn't release her. "That was just a taste of what is to come. Marry me, Aven."

Aven's lips trembled, her eyes flooded with tears, "Leave me be!" She begged him.

"Leave her be." The reverend hurried towards them.

Archie forcefully pushed her away. "I was just trying to help, Rev, I offered to marry her, she ain't got no one else to provide for her."

The reverend put his arm around Aven. "Go away, Mr. Mitchell, we will take care of the family now."

Archie sneered. "And just how are you gonna do that, Rev? You ain't got no more money'n she has."

"Even so, we don't need your help, thank you." The reverend despised Archie Mitchell, but his love for the Lord meant he vowed to treat all people with respect.

Archie scratched at his rough beard. "You'll realise you need me sooner or later. Mark my words."

The reverend ignored his words and led Aven away. Archie turned and walked in the other direction, seething.

Out of sight of the town the reverend stopped walking. "Are you alright?"

Aven's face paled and she took two steps and threw up. Wiping her face on her apron she burst into tears.

Reverend Cartwright embraced the sobbing girl, rubbing his hands up and down her back. "It's alright, he's gone." When she finally calmed he pushed her from him and passed her his clean handkerchief. "Did he hurt you?"

Aven nodded. "He kissed me roughly, I couldn't get away from him." Her lips trembled and her eyes flooded with tears again.

The reverend gently touched her elbow. "I'm sorry, Aven. That's the last thing you need."

Aven nodded. "He's been trying to get me to marry him since I was fifteen."

The reverend nodded. "You're not the only one. He's tried this before."

"Can't someone run him out of town?"

"I'm afraid he's broken no laws, he owns the mill. He's the wealthiest man in this town as far as I know."

"He makes my skin crawl."

The reverend nodded again. "I know, we'll make sure he doesn't get near you. Come on, let's get you home."

Aven gave the clergyman a brave smile. "Thank you for your kindness to us, Reverend. I mean to do whatever it takes to keep my sisters fed and give them a good life."

Reverend Cartwright smiled, took back his handkerchief and they walked toward the Miller homestead. "I know you do, you're a brave strong young woman, Aven, but everyone needs help from time to time. We'll do what we can to help."

"Thank you, I know all this sadness is hard on you too, having to be so strong for all these hurting people."

The reverend stroked his short beard. "That's very astute of you. Yes, it is hard, but it's why the Lord put me here, to minister to all the needs of this town, physical and spiritual. He'll give me the strength."

Aven merely nodded.

"He'll give you the strength too and show you how to get by if you lean on him."

Aven smiled. "I know, thank you."

"You're welcome." The kind man gave her a reassuring smile.

*   *   *   *

"That's the last of the coffee." Ada grimaced across at Aven.

Aven looked up from the skirt she was adding yet another patch to. "We're out of cornstarch, too."

Ada opened a cupboard and peered inside. "We only have enough flour for a few loaves of bread."

Aven sighed. "I know. And we owe Mr. Jensen money, he won't let us have any more on account."

Ada walked over and sat next to Aven on the threadbare couch. "What are we going to do?"

"I don't know, yet." Aven lay down the mending and looked her sister in the eye. "But I promise you, I'll do whatever it takes to make sure you and Amelia are taken care of. I promised Mama when she got sick I'd look after you all." She nodded determinedly. "First things first, I have to find a proper job. We can't keep living on taking in laundry and bits of sewing."

"But where?"

Aven grimaced. Respectable jobs for unmarried women were few in their town. She sighed loudly, lowering her voice as Amelia walked into the room. "I don't know yet, but I give you my word, I will keep us together and I will make sure you have what you need..." She closed her eyes and fought the shudder as a horrific thought crossed her mind. "No matter what I have to do." Her voice petered out. *Please Lord, don't let it come to that. I can't imagine anything worse.*

"What are you two talking about?" Amelia plonked herself down onto the stool before the fire.

"Nothing that concerns you." Aven abruptly changed the subject. "You're miles behind in arithmetic, you must do all the pages I've marked today."

Amelia groaned and rolled her eyes. Thrusting herself back in the chair she punched the couch. "Do I have to?"

"Yes, you have to."

"But what's the point now?"

Aven frowned. "What do you mean?"

The younger girl curled her face up. "Papa's gone, Mama's gone, we ain't got much hope, what's the point of doing schoolwork now?"

Aven reached her hands out to her sister's shoulders and gave her a determined smile. "Amelia, it's more important now than ever. Remember what Papa said? You need to do your studies, to be a smart and educated woman with many possibilities in your life. He wanted a better life for us girls than he had."

Amelia sniffed and shrugged. "How are we gonna do that now without Papa?"

Aven glanced at Ada and then back at her younger sister. "I don't have all the details worked out yet, darling, but I promise you this, I will take care of you and Ada. I will keep us together. I will do all I can to see you have the kind of life Papa always wanted you to have and that means you have to keep up your studies. Who knows what you could be capable of in the future if you get a good education."

Amelia blinked twice, then nodded and threw her arms around her sister's neck. "We will make him proud."

"That's my girl." Aven smiled as her sister stepped back. "I have great hopes for you, sweet girl." She leaned forward and kissed her sister on the forehead.

"But I could work and help to get some money."

Ada and Aven cut her off, both declaring, "No way!"

"Absolutely not!" Aven insisted. "I will find a way to keep the house going and you both cared for, but you are not to worry about that. Okay? All Papa and Mama ever wanted for you was a happy life and education is the most important thing for you now, because education opens up opportunities."

Amelia frowned, but nodded and gave her sister a resigned smile. "Alright, but I still want to help."

"I know, darling." Aven's eyes twinkled for a moment. "You can start by doing the dishes."

Amelia screwed up her face and scowled at her sister, then her face widened into a bright smile. "Sure." She returned her sister's kiss and strode into the kitchen, where Ada had the hot water in a basin ready for the task.

Ada glanced up at her younger sister then back at Aven. She lowered her voice. "What will you do?"

Aven rubbed her chin. "I'll ask around tomorrow. There has to be something I can do to make some money."

"I could come with you."

Aven shook her head. "No, you stay here with Amelia, make sure she gets her schoolwork done and keep the house."

"But I can work?"

"I know, and you can keep on with the stitchin' jobs we have while you're here. I'll ask around if there is anything else available you can do from home."

Ada nodded. "Alright. I pray you find something."

"I will." Aven turned back to her mending pile and concentrated on the task while praying fervently for the Lord's help.

Five

Austen Hart led his lame horse into the small town, spotting the rough sign above the livery stable he sighed in relief. "Come on, Princess, let's get your foot seen to, then we'll work on getting ourselves some food and rest."

The horse gave him a snort, and stumbled along behind him, finally entering the livery.

Mr. Thomas Franklin put down his rake and turned to see who was approaching. He gave the weary stranger a smile and put out a dirty hand to shake. "Good day."

Austen took the hand, ignoring the dirt on it. "Good day, Sir. You know about horses?"

Mr. Franklin smirked. "Some." That was an understatement, there wasn't a man in the town that knew more about horses and most other animals.

Austen nodded. "Austen Hart."

"Tom Franklin." The liveryman was a man of few words, he was a bachelor in his late forties and somewhat bashful. He found his solace in animals rather than people. "Call me Franky."

Austen nodded. "Princess threw a shoe and she's lame. Any chance you could take a look at her. We have a long way to go."

Franky nodded, the man's business was not his concern. He approached the chestnut horse and stroked her nose. Princess nuzzled the man, instinctively knowing he was a kindred spirit. The liveryman walked away and returned with a bucket of chaff and the hungry, weary horse immediately dipped her head in it. The man stroked the horse's neck again and ran his hand down her injured leg, the horse lifted her head and gave a little snort as he examined her lower leg and hoof. The man petted her again. "It's okay, girl." He put the hoof back down and looked up at Austen. "She's lame alright."

Austen nodded. "Can you help her?"

"Yeah, but she'll not be right for some time. She wouldn't have made it much further."

Austen grimaced. "What're you saying? How long till she comes right?"

The man continued to stroke the horse's neck while he spoke. "Hard to say, her foot's in a bad way, it appears she has worms and needs better feed." Franky shrugged. "A month, give or take."

Austen grimaced again. "Blast! We hoped to make California before the snows come."

Franky took the empty chaff bucket and brought the horse some water. "Won't be going nowhere on this horse."

Austen sighed. "Perhaps this is an excuse for a break."

"You could get yourself another horse."

"I couldn't, Princess and me have been together a long time. I'll do what it takes to get her well." Austen's eyes grew far away and a slight shadow crossed his face. "She saved my life." His voice became dreamy.

Franky merely nodded. "Leave her here, I'll take care of her."

"Much obliged, Sir." He reached into his pocket and pulled out a few banknotes, passed the man five dollars and shoved the rest back into his pocket. "Will this cover it?"

"That'll more'n do." The man nodded and tucked the note into his own pocket.

"Can you tell me where I can stay in this town?" Austen removed the horse's saddle and lifted his saddle bag satchel and small carpet bag over his shoulder.

"There's a boarding house or the saloon." Franky gestured towards town.

Austen nodded. "Much obliged." He smiled, stroked Princess's nose and strode in the direction Franky had pointed him.

He took a deep breath and looked around at the small town as he walked. *Peaceful little town.* He doffed his hat at a woman passing by. "Good day, Ma'am." He noticed her black garments and observed that she was with child. He gave her a sympathetic smile. The woman returned his smile although her haunted expression told the man her grief was very recent. He shook his head as he walked away. *Poor woman.* He sighed in relief when he reached the boarding house. *I can't wait for a warm bath and a soft bed.*

He walked into the foyer and a sign on the wall above a bell said 'ring for assistance' so he rang the bell.

A cheerful middle-aged woman walked out, drying her hands on her apron. "Good day." She smiled.

"Ma'am." Austen returned her smile. "Need a room if I may, Miss?"

"Mrs." She smiled. "Mrs. Samantha Grant." The woman nodded and walked over to a small table where there was a ledger. She opened the leather-bound book and took the ink pen from the inkwell "What's ya name?"

"Hart."

She nodded. "You on your own, Mr. Hart?"

He smiled. "Yes, Ma'am."

"How long you planning to stay?"

"I'm not certain, could be several weeks, maybe longer." He grimaced slightly without meaning to. This delay could set him back months. His sister was expecting him in California.

"Very good, two bits a day. I serve breakfast and supper, you gotta see to ya own noon meal. This town has a small café and the saloon, both offer a midday meal."

Austen nodded. "Thank you, Ma'am." He reached into his pocket and passed the woman a bank note. "This should cover it, if I'm here longer I'll get you some more."

The woman's brows raised as she gripped the five dollar bill. *Don't look a gift horse in the mouth, Samantha, just be grateful.* She jotted down, 'Room 7' in the ledger next to his name. It was their best room, she usually saved it for important guests. "Right this way, Mr. Hart." She gestured to the hallway as she poked the bank note in her pocket.

Austen followed the woman down the long hallway and up a staircase to the second floor. She led him to a room with a balcony, overlooking the street. It had a large bed in the middle, a small desk with a mirror above it and a stuffed chair. In the corner was a little settee with a low table next to it. The room also had a tall robe and an armoire in the corner. Austen looked around and smiled. It was a pretty room.

Mrs. Grant walked in and pulled back the long drapes. She pushed open the wide doors out onto the balcony. "This here's our best room." She smiled. "Got ya own private balcony here." She'd inherited the house from her late husband who was the town's founder and the owner of the large mill until she'd sold it after he died to make ends meet. This had been their bedroom in their large home before she'd turned their home into a boarding house.

Her three children had long left their town and were off living lives of their own in cities far away that she'd never seen. But Samantha was content with her busy boarding house and her quiet life on the Montana Plains.

"Much obliged, Ma'am." Austen lay his saddle bag and satchel on top of the armoire and smiled at the woman.

"Supper is at seven, bathroom is at the end of the hall."

Austen nodded and was unable to stifle a yawn. He pulled out his silver pocket watch and flicked it open as the woman headed out of the room. "Four fifteen. Time for a bath and a rest before supper."

Austen wandered down the stairs in clean clothing, fresh shaven and well-rested. He nodded to the two men, and three women who shared the dining room with him. He smiled as he noticed the young widow he'd seen earlier walk out with a heavy pot of stew. He gasped and leapt up. "Let me help you with that, Ma'am." He put his hands on the sides of the pot.

She frowned but then nodded and passed him the pot. "Thank you." She smiled.

"My pleasure." He put the pot on the table where the woman gestured. "Anything else you need help with?" Austen smiled kindly. He observed the weariness in her face and grimaced, hoping she wasn't overdoing it.

"No this is the last of it, thank you." She untied her apron and took a seat as Mrs. Grant arrived behind her with a large pot of potatoes.

They took their seats and the meal began. Austen took his first bite and his stomach reminded him it had been a long time since he'd had a homecooked meal. He smiled at Mrs. Grant. "This is delicious, thank you, Ma'am."

She nodded and gave him a smile. "There's plenty, so eat all ya want." She gestured to pots of food on the table before them.

He nodded and scooped a potato onto his fork and shoved it in his mouth. He looked around at the pretty room and the others who shared the table. His eyes fell on the young widow again and he was moved with compassion for her. *About six months along I'd guess.*

Mrs. Grant took the time to observe the kind stranger. He was tall, with a crop of dark, nearly black hair, kind blue eyes and a square jaw. He had a presence about him, a quiet, determined strength of character despite the cloud that seemed to hang over him. His clothing suggested he wasn't poor, yet he didn't have much with him, unless his possessions were to follow.

A fellow across from him put his fork down. "So, Mr. Hart, what brings you to our town?

Austen smiled and took a sip of his coffee. "I'm headed to California. Mr?"

"Lohan."

Austen nodded.

"What's in California." The young widow asked.

Austen smiled. "My sister is there with her husband."

"In the gold fields?" Mrs. Grant asked.

Austen curled up one side of his mouth and nodded. "Yeah."

Mr. Lohan raised his brows. "You a prospector?"

"Not yet." He smiled.

All eyes swung toward the doorway as a young woman walked in carrying a basket, clad in black clothing. "Oh, excuse me, I thought your supper

35

would be over." Aven grimaced. Her eyes flicked to Austen's and she gave him a wry smile.

Mrs. Grant stood up. "Never mind, Miss Miller."

"I've brought your curtains by."

Mrs. Grant nodded. "Come on into the kitchen. I've got ya money."

Aven followed the woman out of the room.

Austen observed the woman. She seemed to be no more than eighteen if he guessed. Based on her black dress he imagined she'd also lost someone close to her. She had a kind face but there was a darkness behind her blue eyes. *There is so much sadness in this town.*

He watched as the two women walked past the dining room to the foyer. They stopped walking as they reached the door, unaware that their voices traveled to the dining room

"Thank you, Mrs. Grant." The young woman clutched her now empty basket and smiled. "Might you have any more work for me?"

Austen heard Mrs. Grant sigh. "I wish I did. You know I have Miranda Watson working here now. I can barely afford to pay her."

Aven sucked in a breath. "Thank you. You've been most kind."

Mrs. Grant put her hand on Aven's arm. "I'm sorry, I wish I could help you, especially with your sisters to care for. I'll ask around for ya. You're a good worker and your stitchin' is excellent. I can't fault ya there."

Aven nodded. "I appreciate it. Now I must get home, I have to repair the canvas on Mr. Franklin's wagon tonight, he needs it for tomorrow morning."

Mrs. Grant gave her a compassionate smile and a nod. "I'll leave you to it then."

Aven nodded and with a loud sigh she left the boarding house.

Austen watched Mrs. Grant walk back in and resume her spot. *That young woman has a very hard time of it. I wish I knew who she was and if there was a way to help her.*

Mrs. Grant put her fork down and hung her head. Austen looked up at her. "Is everything alright, Ma'am?"

She managed a slight smile. "Yes, it's just there is a lot of sadness in this town." She turned to Miranda, the young widow and gripped her hand. "I wish I could do more to help."

Austen turned his eyes from the older woman's face to the young widow. She wasn't much older than the woman who had just left. She gave Mrs. Grant a smile. "I'm so grateful to you for giving me work here, Mrs. Grant. I don't know what might have happened to us if you didn't take me in." She put her hand on her growing baby.

Mrs. Grant patted the woman's forearm. "Least I c'n do, 'specially with ya being in the family way and all."

Miranda's eyes flooded with tears and she concentrated on her meal again.

Austen squinted his eyes. He didn't want to pry but was filled with compassion for these people. *I wonder what happened?*

Six

Aven arose from her bed before the old rooster had even warmed up his vocal cords. She dressed as quickly and quietly as she could so as not to wake her sisters sleeping in the next room. She pinned up her hair and stood to stretch her sore muscles. She lifted her lantern and poked her head in her sister's room. They were both fast asleep. She was grateful for that.

She hurried into her coat and boots, picked up her basket and headed out into the dark and cold of the early morning. She lifted the lantern before her and walked all the way to town. Their gig had a broken wheel, and she couldn't carry her basket on horseback. The walk wasn't so bad, at least it wasn't raining this morning.

Reaching the saloon she knocked at the door. It was some time before the bartender, 'Whiskey Jim', opened the double doors. "Mornin'" he managed gruffly. "Ya early."

"I'm sorry, Jim. I need to get finished before my sisters wake up."

"Very well." He nodded, gestured her inside and shut the door. "I'll get ya money and ya can see yaself out when ya finished."

Aven nodded as he hurried into his small back room. *He's not nearly as gruff as he makes himself out to be.* She smiled as she lay her basket on the counter and lifted the large copper pot onto the stove. Finding a pitcher she filled it with water from the pump and, a pitcher at a time, she filled the copper.

Whiskey Jim wandered back out and placed two quarters on the counter. He gave her a smile. "Fifty cents, like I promised. Ya do a good job and we could make this a weekly thing." He felt sorry for the girl. He had three younger sisters, living back east with his mother and father, and he couldn't imagine what it would be like for them having to fend for themselves. Respectable work was scarce for a woman in their town so he was happy to do what he could to help. He hadn't owned the saloon long and their town's ban on woman entertaining in the saloon, meant he didn't make as much as other saloon owners might. But he could manage fifty cents for the girl. She saved him a huge job.

Aven nodded her thanks and fetched a mop and bucket from a small cupboard near the stove. The clock struck four as she poured the hot water into the bucket, added a pitcher fill of cool water and went to work scrubbing every inch of the saloon, floor, tables and even the windows.

"Ma'am.... Wake up."

Aven jolted awake to a person shaking her. She lifted her head and looked around. She bit her lip and leapt up. "Oh, I'm sorry, Jim. I only sat down for a few minutes to rest my eyes."

Whiskey Jim smiled. "'t's alright, no harm done." He looked around at the now light saloon, the sun was rising and light streamed in the gleaming windows. "Ya did a good job, place ain't looked this clean since I brought it,"

She smiled. "Thank you." She caught a glimpse at the clock behind him and gasped loudly. "Oh no, I'm late."

Jim nodded and watched as she snatched the coins off the counter, threw the dirty rags in her basket to take home to wash and hurried out the door. She had one more job to do before she got home.

Aven helped Franky lace the canvas to his wagon. He smiled. "Ya did a fine job, neatest patch I seen."

"Thank you, it should hold."

The man nodded. "It'll hold. Ya work is good."

"Thank you, and I thank you for the work. Might you have more? I'll do anything that needs to be done, even muck out stables if ya want me to."

Franky shook his head. "That's no work for a woman, sides I got the young Elliot boy working for me. Lost his pa too and needs the work." He gave her a contrite look. "I'm sorry I can't do more for ya."

Aven nodded. "That's okay, I thank you for this job."

"I'll get ya money." The man hurried into his small home behind the livery and returned with a few coins. "I'm giving ya ten cents extra for the fine work, and done at short notice."

Aven knew she should protest and give back the extra money, but she remembered the reverend's kind words to her a few days earlier. "There is no harm in charity, it's good for a person to give and to receive."

"Thank you, Franky." She sniffed away the threatening emotion.

The man merely nodded and turned to greet the approaching man.

Austen recognized Aven and gave her a kind smile. She nodded and hurried away. He returned Franky's handshake and turned his head back to watch the retreating woman. "She seems awful determined."

Franky nodded and stroked at his beard. "A lot'a sadness in this town." He shook his head and strode into the livery.

Austen followed him. "What happened?"

Franky flicked a bridle from a hook on the wall and walked into the first pen. He reached up to stroke the nose of his draft horse, Clyde, and lifted the bit to the horse's mouth. "Was about a month back, lost five good men in a logging accident."

"Was her husband one?"

Franky shook his head. "Her pa, ma's been gone 'most a year, got two young sisters to look after."

A wave of compassion ran through Austen, so strong it nearly knocked him off his feet. "How tragic. Is that what took the husband of the young widow, Watson, I think was her name."

"Yes." Franky frowned. "And the pa of the lad who works for me. Lots'a sadness." He shook his head. "Wish there was more I could do."

Austen nodded. "How's she making ends meet?"

"Mrs. Watson is working at the boarding house."

Austen smirked. "No, I mean the young woman that just left here."

"Odd jobs where she can get 'em. Works hard and tends to their property too. If she's not careful she'll collapse."

"I suppose she's doing what's necessary to keep her family together."

"Yes, she's a hard worker, a brave and resilient woman. Life's dealt her many cruel blows." The man led the horse out to his waiting wagon. "I'm headed out to the Turner estate to look at some horses, is there something you need, Mr. Hart?"

"I just came to check on Princess."

"She's on the mend, some way to go yet though." He gestured back into the livery. "Don't put no weight on her foot yet."

"I won't I just want to see she's faring alright."

The livery man gestured to the open door and leapt up on the wagon seat. "Be seeing ya."

"Much obliged." Austen waved and walked inside to check on Princess.

* * * *

Ada poked her head out the door. "Aven, breakfast is ready."

Aven nodded. "I'll just finish pulling these carrots, I have to get them to Mr. Sullivan. He's offered me two rabbits in exchange for these vegetables."

Ada screwed up her nose as she walked inside. She'd never cared for rabbit, but they weren't in any position to be picky, they ate whatever they could get. "I'm glad we put in a large garden that we have

43

enough to trade. Thank you, Lord." She chose to be grateful.

Aven walked in and placed her basket down, she hurried over to the basin in the kitchen and dipped her hands in the warm water.

Ada noticed her older sister grimace. "Amelia, will you finish setting the table," she asked and strode over to her Aven. "Ohhh, Aven, your hands."

Aven lifted blistered, red hands from the water and grimaced. "I'll be alright."

"At least let me put some salve on them." Ada hurried to the pantry and pulled out the salve. Aven groaned as her sister rubbed the ointment in into her blistered hands.

"Thank you." Aven gave her sister a grateful smile.

"Ave, you are working too hard, you can't keep this up."

"I have to." Aven shrugged determinedly. "I promised I'd keep us all together and fed and I mean to."

"But I could work, too, take some of the pressure off you."

"No, I won't hear of it." Aven's voice was stern. "I need you here to look after the house and Amelia."

Ada shrugged. "At least let me take the eggs to the store each day, save you one job at least. We could make it Amelia's arithmetic project, adding the cost and keeping a ledger."

Aven nodded. "Alright, but it's more important to me that the two of you get your studies. I'm determined you'll have a better life than me."

Ada gave in. "Alright, come on, let's have breakfast."

* * * *

Austen made his way to a small lake. A log had been moved near the water and the worn bark suggested many people had sat there over the years. He took his seat, pulled an apple from his pocket and sat down. His mind grew far away as he thought about the town and the circumstances of him ending up there. "What do you have planned for me, Lord?" He raised his eyes to the heavens. "This certainly wasn't where I expected to be."

His thoughts tumbled over themselves and his mind drifted back to the events of a year ago. A recent graduate of Harvard Medical school, his life was everything he'd hoped. He graduated with excellent grades and had won a job at a prestigious hospital near his parent's home in New York City. He had a lovely fianceé and his future looked bright.

Austen sighed loudly and closed his eyes. "But I couldn't save her." He shook his head. All his up to date medical knowledge could not save Harriet from the cancer that ravaged her body. "What good is having a medical degree if I can't save the people I love?" He sniffed back a sob.

The day Harriet had died he walked out of the hospital, hung up his stethoscope and never went back. He walked to the saloon and drank himself into a stupor. While intoxicated he was robbed and, dragged out into the forest by a group of thugs where they beat him within an inch of his life..

It was there that Princess had found him. She wasn't a wild horse, that was obvious, but she'd lived in the woods for a time. He'd woken up to the horse nudging him. He'd tried to sit up but couldn't. He could barely lift himself. Instinctively the horse sat down and Austen managed with a colossal effort to pull himself up onto her back. He clung to her neck and she stood carefully and wandered into town. A man stopped the horse and helped Austen to the hospital, the very room Harriet had died in.

The moment he was up and about again he vowed to get out of the city. He purchased a saddle and bridle, sold all but his most prized possessions and Princess and he headed west.

His sister's husband had struck a large vein of gold in California and was doing very well. There was a place there for Austen if he wanted it. He couldn't explain why he hadn't taken the train and stage.

Perhaps he just wanted to be alone with his thoughts. He scratched his chin and stared at the lake. He'd left New York several months ago and slowly made his way west. He had no time frame in mind except he hoped to arrive before the snows covered the prairies and made the going twice as hard. Along the way he'd found odd jobs in small towns. In one such town, Red Fern on the banks of Lake Erie he'd met Pastor Elliot Smythe who had introduced him to God. He was new to this idea of relying on God but he was thankful. He knew that it was God who guided his steps.

He'd spent a lot of time thinking about Harriet and medicine and all that had happened. He took solace in God and in Princess who'd been his faithful companion for the entire journey. Sometimes he'd travelled with wagons and other sojourners but most of the time it was just he and Princess.

He took a deep breath and raised his eyes to the heavens again. This was the first time in months he'd felt light-hearted. Something about this town had ministered to his heart. Maybe it was knowing that the people here had faced as much tragedy as he had and yet they carried on so bravely despite it. "If they can, I can." He nodded and bowed his head to pray.

"Lord, help me. I need to let Harriet go and live again."

"I AM with you." A small voice in his heart spoke. He smiled and nodded. "Yes, You are with me. I have no idea what to do next, but I trust You'll show me."

Seven

Aven stood and stretched her back. She wiped her wrist across her forehead and sighed. Moving further down the row she bent over again and pulled out more carrots, as many as she could reach before moving again. Her basket was almost filled with vegetables. She stood and sighed again looking across the garden one way and then back the way she'd come. She was more than halfway through the task. Pausing for a moment Aven lifted her canteen to her mouth, wiped the remaining drips off her face, replaced the lid and put her canteen back down. She shrugged her shoulders, exhaled loudly and bent over again desperately fighting the urge to collapse. "Come on Aven, you've got to do this. Mr. Cooper offered us ten cents a bushel," she encouraged herself. Lifting her head slightly she looked at the back of wagon. It held at least two bushels and the garden still had a couple more bushels worth of vegetables in it. "I could earn fifty maybe even sixty cents for this job. That would go a long way to paying our debt at the mercantile."

Every muscle in her body ached and she was hopelessly tired. *But I can't quit. I need to work. Mr. Cooper may have more work for me after this.* She wiped her brow with her apron and placed two more handfuls of carrots into the basket. It was about as full as she could manage to carry so she gripped the basket and walked with it to the wagon, slid it on next to the other baskets and fetched an empty one.

The clock on the bank struck the hour and she exhaled deeply again and carried the basket back to the vegetable patch to continue the task.

*   *   *   *

Ada lifted the last dish from the soapy water and handed it to Amelia to dry. The little girl wiped out the dish and Ada cast a furtive glance at the clock. Amelia caught it. "Aven's really late."

"She'll be here soon."

Amelia nodded but her lip trembled and her eyes filled with tears.

"What is it?"

Amelia placed down the dish and looked up at Ada. "When Papa was this late it was because he had died."

Ada closed her eyes and blew her breath out loudly. "Don't say that. Aven will be just fine, darling, she's just working hard is all".

"What if Aven dies, too?"

"Amelia, she's only picking vegetables, how could she die from that?"

Amelia shrugged. "I don't..." Her voice was cut off by footsteps on the porch. Both girls looked towards the door. "Aven? Her face fell when she heard a pounding on the door. Aven wouldn't knock at her own home. The little girl paused and a sense of terror filled her.

49

"Come on, open the door." Aven's tired voice could barely be heard.

Amelia gasped. "Aven." She bolted to the door, and Ada hurried over.

Aven staggered in, thrust her basket in Ada's hands and collapsed onto the sofa.

Neither of her sister's moved. Ada looked down at the basket and back up her sister. "What's this?" She gestured to the vegetables and few pantry staples in the basket.

Aven lay along the couch and lay her head on the armrest. "What's it look like?" Her voice was barely more than a whisper.

"Food? Amelia smiled.

Ada walked to the kitchen and put the basket on the counter. "Where did you get all this?"'

"Mr. Cooper." Aven's eyes were tightly closed and her words labored as though if she spoke them aloud they'd tire her out.

Ada gasped and still holding a carrot in her hand she marched out to stand before the couch. "You didn't..." She bit her lip. "Nevermind."

one eye and glared at her sister. "I didn't steal them if that's what you mean."

"I know you wouldn't do that. I'm just surprised. I thought Mr. Cooper was going to give you cash money?"

Aven took a deep breath and sat up. "He did, then he said I could have a basketful of vegetables. I used some of the money to buy flour, sugar and coffee. The rest I gave to Mr. Hansen for our account."

Ada nodded and hurried to the kitchen to unpack the basket.

Amelia looked down and noticed Aven's hands. "Ohhh, your hands are shaking."

Aven shrugged. "I'm just tired."

"You've worked so hard." The little girl sounded contrite.

Ada finished her job, poured some coffee in a cup and held it out to Aven.

"Thank you." Aven took a long slurp and held the coffee between her hands.

Ada nodded and sat down beside Aven. "Are you sure you aren't overdoing it? I could work too?" She pleaded.

Aven squared her shoulders and frowned at Ada. "No, I've told you, I want you and Amelia to get an education. Besides you do all the work around here."

Ada nodded, there was no point arguing.

"I don't mind working hard." Aven took another long draft of the coffee. "I just wish there was a way I could earn more, no one wants to pay a woman much."

Ada screwed up her face. "It isn't fair, you worked hard today."

"And he gave me fifty cents. But we still owe Mr. Hansen more than three dollars. Amelia desperately needs a new dress, and I'm not sure how much longer we can keep repairing our stockings." *And Amelia's birthday is coming up.* Aven hid her grimace by draining her cup.

Ada reached for her empty cup. "You want more?"

Aven shook her head.

"You want some supper?"

"No, I think I'll just take a bath and go to bed. I have to be at the saloon early."

"We've already got the copper full and lit. We figured you'd want a bath." Amelia smiled.

"Thank you," Aven managed and pushed herself slowly up from the chair. "I can't wait to get my feet out of these shoes and into the warm water."

Ada nodded. "I bet. You go have your bath, I'll bring your nightclothes and a clean towel."

Aven gave her sisters a weak smile. "Check on me in fifteen minutes, in case I've fallen asleep."

"I will." Amelia smiled.

Eight

Austen strolled out the boardinghouse door and stopped to speak to the young woman washing the front windows. "Good morning, Ma'am."

Aven paused and turned to look at him. "Good morning." She gave him a tired smile and turned back to her task. It was her third job of the morning and it wasn't yet eight.

Austen's doctor eyes examined the woman. She was pale and thin, and her face displayed fatigue. He scrambled in his mind for something to say to her. "Lovely weather isn't it?"

Aven nodded but didn't turn her eyes from the window. "mmmhmmm." She murmured.

Austen nodded, she was busy and he should leave her to it. "Good day." He smiled, put his hat on his head and began to walk away.

Aven's head swirled she stopped and wiped her arm across her forehead. She closed her eyes and with a deep sigh she collapsed on the boardwalk knocking over her water bucket, sending soapy water over the wooden boards and down onto the dusty road.

Austen heard her sigh. He turned to look at her and gasped as he saw her faint.

"Ma'am." He hurried to her. "Ma'am, can you hear me?" He scooped her up and carried her into the dining room. "Help me!" he called.

Mrs. Grant hurried out of the kitchen and gasped. "Oh, Miss Miller." She glanced at the doctor as he placed her in a chair in the sitting room. "What happened?"

Austen knelt before her. "She fainted, poor girl, I think she's exhausted." He tried hard to sound like a caring citizen rather than a doctor.

"I'll get a cool cloth." Mrs. Grant hurried away.

With no one looking Austen examined the girl as best he could. She groaned and he squeezed her arm. "Ma'am. Can you hear me? Ma'am?"

She groaned again and turned her head to the side.

"Ma'am." Austen patted her hand. "It's going to be alright. You're alright." He nodded to Mrs. Grant and took the cold cloth from her hands. He held it to Aven's hot forehead and cheeks. She groaned again and her eyes fluttered. "Ma'am, that's it, Ma'am," he spoke soothingly to her.

Aven whimpered and opened her eyes. "What.... Wha..."

Austen smiled and held the cool cloth to her forehead. "You fainted, Miss Miller." He examined her face as she came around.

"Oh..." Aven raised her hand to her head.

"How are you feeling?" Mrs. Grant asked.

"Dizzy," Aven managed, closing her eyes and leaning her head back.

"You need to rest."

Aven opened her eyes and shook her head. "I have to work."

Austen touched her arm gently. "Miss Miller, you can't keep going like this, you're obviously exhausted."

"I'll get you some water." Mrs. Green hurried out.

"I have to work." Aven insisted. "For my sisters." She grimaced as her head continued to spin.

"When was the last time you ate?"

"We only had enough flour for pancakes for the girls. So, I just had coffee for breakfast, but that was at four o'clock, I had to be at the saloon by five."

Mrs. Grant entered the room and thrust the glass of water at her.

Aven nodded and took it. She sipped at it. "I'll be alright, I just got so hot. I should drink more water!"

"You must eat, Miss Miller, and you can't work so hard, you'll collapse and then you'll not be able to work at all," Mrs. Grant implored her.

Tears sprung to the corners of her eyes and she bit her lip. "I have to. How else will we make ends meet? We're already in debt to Mr. Hansen and at the bank, and are behind in our house payments. Mr. Cooper won't keep providing us vegetables." Aven shrugged. "I have to work."

Austen felt a wave of compassion run through him. "Is there a way you can get a job that doesn't wear you out so much?"

"Where?" Aven drained her cup. "As it is I've only been able to find odd jobs, but most of the people in this town are poor and can barely afford to pay anything."

Mrs. Grant gave her a compassionate smile. "I'll get ya something to eat and you can sit there for a time."

"I can't pay you for it?" Aven grimaced. "But you could take it out of my pay."

Mrs. Grant frowned. "You don't need to pay for it, and I'll not be taking a cent from your pay. I offered you fifty cents to wash all the windows and I'll not be going back on that. I'm sure we can spare a little food for you." Mrs. Grant wasn't a wealthy woman but she felt sorry for Aven and could find a little now and then to let Aven work sometimes, but she was acutely aware of the dwindling funds in her own account.

Aven felt her stomach rumble and realized just how hungry she was. She'd given the majority of the food to her sisters only ate sparingly. "No. Thank you, Mrs. Grant. We don't need charity. I just want to work to earn enough to feed my sisters." Her voice trembled and a tear spilled from her eye and streaked down her cheek.

Austen closed his eyes and sighed. *What a hard life this young woman has.* He determined in his mind he would do what he could to help her. But she was proud and wouldn't take charity so he'd have to play this carefully, and without exposing the fact that he was a doctor.

Mrs. Grant stepped closer and gripped Aven's shoulder. "Everyone needs a little charity now and again, Miss Miller, ain't nothing wrong with that."

Aven meant to protest again but Austen looked at her and raised his eyebrows. "Think of it this way, if you knew of someone who was hungry and exhausted and you had the means to help them, wouldn't you do what you could?"

Aven closed her eyes and took a deep breath. She managed a wry smile. "Yes. I would."

Mrs. Grant smiled. "I'll get ya something to eat, and some coffee."

Aven could do little more than nod.

Austen gave her a kind smile and stood up. "You'll be alright now, but you have to find a way to slow down some, get some sleep and proper nutrition."

Aven frowned. "You are kind, but you don't get it. We don't have a lot and Papa left us with a small debt to pay and no savings." She shrugged. "All the money he had went to pay for Mama's medical treatment." Aven swiped at a tear that threatened. "It was all for nothing, she died anyway."

Austen closed his eyes and shuddered. He turned to look out the window briefly and take a deep breath. He knew that feeling only too well. He turned back to her. "I'm sorry. What a tragic thing to lose both your parents like that."

Aven nodded and gave him an appreciative smile. "We mustn't question God. He is sovereign. We can only do the best we can with what he provides. That's what I'm trying to do, Sir."

Austen nodded. "Please, just call me Austen."

Aven nodded. "And I'd like it if you called me Aven or Miss Miller, not Ma'am. That always makes me feel so old."

Austen nodded again and Mrs. Grant entered the room. "I've got some oatmeal and coffee for you, Miss. Can ya stand? Come into the dining room?"

Aven nodded and pressed her hands against the side of the chair. She pushed herself up and her head swirled so she paused.

"Let me help you." Austen lunged forward, put his arm around her waist and helped her to stand.

"Thank you," Aven whispered, shrugging off his hands when she was steady on her feet. "I can walk." She turned and walked away, determinedly holding her head up.

Austen smiled and shook his head as he watched her walk away. *She is a stubborn and determined young woman.* He found her intriguing and admired the way she had determinedly taken on the role of provider for her family. Austen scratched at his chin and followed her to the dining room. Mrs. Grant had a tray of muffins on the table along with the coffee pot and three cups so they poured themselves each a cup and sat down with Aven.

Mrs. Grant gestured to the bowl. "Eat all that oatmeal, Aven, it'll do ya good."

"Thank you." Aven's growling stomach overruled her principles and she began to eat it.

"Don't eat too much too quickly," Austen added. "If you've not had much in your stomach it can make you sick. And take plenty of water with it."

Mrs. Grant squinted at Austen and swallowed her mouthful of muffin. "How do you know so much about caring for folks?"

Austen shrugged and slurped at his coffee as he formed an answer. "I uh... I've just learned things in my travels." He offered.

Mrs. Grant squinted again but nodded.

The trio shared small talk while they ate, and Austen took the time to observe the girl. Despite the disheveled hair and dirt on her clothing, the tiredness of her face and her somewhat callused hands, she was very beautiful. He smiled as he considered how very different she was to Harriet.

Harriet was a wealthy socialite who spent her days in drawing rooms and cotillions. He'd loved her, she was beautiful and caring in her own way. She just knew no better than a wealthy New York life. *But I left that world, and I won't ever go back to it.* It wasn't that he was ungrateful. The life of privilege he'd led meant he'd got a good education. Still, he couldn't shake the secrets from his past. He hoped that moving west, he would at last be able to let New York go, once and for all, and leave Harriet in the past where she belonged. A lovely memory of a lost love.

Aven's words broke through his musings.

"Thank you, Mrs. Grant. I need to get back to work now."

Austen raised his brows at her. "Are you sure?"

Aven thrust her chin out. "I'm fine."

Both Mrs. Grant and Austen furrowed their brows.

"I promise to slow down a bit. But I have to work."

The other two looked at each other and back at Aven and nodded.

Aven cleaned her bowl and stood.

Austen stood at the same time, as a gentleman did for a lady.

Aven instinctively reached for her bowl. Mrs. Grant touched her arm. "Leave the dishes, love, I'll take care'a 'em. Get back to ya windas." The older woman's voice dripped with compassion.

"Thank you for your kindness."

Mrs. Grant gave her a wide smile and gently squeezed the arm she touched. "I'm glad to help ya howeva I c'n. I'm just sorry I can't give ya more work."

Aven returned her smile. "That's okay, I appreciate what you've done for me." She turned her head and gave Austen a nod.

He nodded in return and smiled as she walked away.

The clock struck midday as Aven carried her pail of very dirty water around the side of the boarding house to the small patch of grass behind. She thrust the water onto a patch of wild daisies and turned to walk back to the front entrance.

"Hello, Miss Miller."

The voice made her squirm and stop dead in her tracks. "Good day, Mr. Mitchell." He blocked the alleyway so she turned and abruptly walked away in the opposite direction.

"Aven, don't walk away from me." The man sneered.

Aven ignored him and kept walking. Mr. Packard at the post office needed someone to deliver some packages. His store boy was sick and Aven had offered her services. He needed her there at precisely one o clock and she just had time to bathe and change her dress.

Archie scowled at her retreating figure and a deep groan came from deep inside his throat. He lunged forward and grabbed Aven by the arm. He spun her around. "I said, don't walk away from me."

Aven tried to keep the fear from her eyes. "I need to go, Mr. Mitchell, I have work to do."

"Work?"

"Yes. I have to work to feed my sisters."

Archie flashed her a wide and smarmy smile. He reached up and tucked some hair behind her ear. "You know, if we married you'd never have to work again."

Aven shuddered and took a step back from him. She swallowed back the snarky retorts and gave him the kindest smile she could muster. "There will be no need, we'll be just fine."

"I'm quite a catch, ain't anyone richer'n me in town."

"Mr. Mitchell, you're old enough to be my father, I'm not interested in marrying you." She tried to keep her voice even.

Archie ran one finger down her cheek. "Age is just a number, Aven. I'd be a good husband to you."

The sinister look in his eye frightened her and she hid her shudder and pulled her head away from him. "I said no." She pivoted on her heels and ran away.

Archie squinted at her and scratched his chin as he watched her hurry away. "I'll get my way." He spoke out loud to himself. "You'll see. She'll be my wife." He sneered. *She's a hard-worker and very young and beautiful. Just what a man like me needs, a woman to take care of the house and all my needs.* "Yes, she'll do nicely."

Nine

"Potatoes?" Aven smiled as Ada put a plate before her. "Where'd you get those?"

"A magic fairy."

Aven frowned at her. "Be serious, Ada."

"We don't know." Amelia placed the coffee pot on the table and slid into a chair opposite her older sister.

Aven bowed her head and gave thanks for the food. Afterwards, she slipped a piece of new potato in her mouth and rolled her eyes back. "Yum." She swallowed it and looked at her sisters. "What do you mean you don't know where the potatoes came from?"

"It means we don't know." Ada shrugged and lifted a very chewy piece of stew to her mouth.

"Well, where did you get them?"

"They were sitting on the porch this morning when I went outside earlier," Amelia said nonchalantly.

Aven frowned. "I wonder where they came from?"

"I don't know." Amelia swallowed her potato and grinned. "Don't look a gift potato in the eye."

Aven and Ada laughed at her unintentional pun.

"You're right, it sure is a treat to have new potatoes." Aven smiled and then yawned.

Amelia frowned. "Tired?"

Aven sighed. "Just a long day is all."

"You work too hard," Ada scolded.

"I have to, Ada, we have to eat. We can't live on gift potatoes forever. Amelia needs new shoes, all our stockings are threadbare and we are in desperate need of new underthings. That all costs money. Not to mention our debts and we have a house payment to make."

"You really should let me work," Ada protested for the umpteenth time.

"Ada, we've been through this and I'm not gonna keep arguing. I need you here, with Amelia."

Ada frowned and nodded. "Alright."

Aven nodded. "Besides you're taking in sewing and that money you make is a big help."

"A few cents here or there." Ada shrugged and shoveled a mouthful of cooked spinach in her mouth. She frowned and swallowed it without chewing. Spinach was her least favorite food, but beggars can't be choosers so she was grateful for what she could get.

"Ada, every little bit helps. Those cents you earn could be the difference between us eating or not." Aven pushed a potato to the side of her plate to save for the end. "I really do appreciate your efforts. It's a huge burden off my shoulders to know our home is being looked after, and Amelia can do her studies. I'm counting on her to make something of herself so she doesn't have to struggle all her days." Aven grimaced. "Not having to come home and make supper means I can work more hours and we all benefit."

"But you're gonna collapse if you don't slow down."

Aven took a sip of her coffee and swallowed back the truth of the morning's fainting spell. "I'll be fine girls. It won't be forever, we'll get our debt paid off then I can ease up a bit."

"Or...." Amelia stopped and bit her lip.

"Or what?" Aven squinted at her.

"Or you could get married to someone with money."

Aven scowled at her. "And just who am I supposed to marry?"

Amelia shrugged. "I dunno, someone, anyone as long as they have money."

"That is not a good reason to get married."

"I know."

"Besides there is no one in this town that has money," Ada added.

"There's Mr. Mitchell," Amelia said.

Aven dropped her fork and scowled at her sister. "I wouldn't marry him if he were the last man on earth and we were desperate. I'd rather starve to death."

"Sorry, I was only joking." Amelia gave her a contrite smile.

"It's okay, darling. I'm not going to marry Mr. Mitchell or any other rich man. I'd rather work hard all my days."

Amelia nodded and the sisters changed the subject.

*　*　*　*

65

Austen strode into the mercantile with his hands in his pockets. He walked around the entire store watching carefully who was in there. He picked up a few items and put them down again. Finally, the last person left and he approached the counter. "Good day, Mr. Hansen."

The store man lifted his head and tucked his pencil behind his ear. "Good day, Mr. Hart, vat can I get ya today?"

"Oh, ahhhh..." Austen looked around to make sure no one was in the store. "I have a rather strange request to make."

"Oh, yes." The older man raised his eyebrows.

Austen leaned in and whispered his request.

*   *   *   *

"You've done a good job, Miss Miller, I ain't never seen my glasses so clean."

Aven smiled at Whiskey Jim as she placed back the last two on the shelf. "Thank you. Ma always taught me to give my best no matter the task. Even when polishing glasses in the saloon."

Whiskey Jim nodded. "Well, I'm grateful to ya. Sorry I can't give ya more work, Miss Miller." The man looked contrite. "I know times are tough for ya."

Aven placed a hand on his arm. "Times are tough for most of the people in this town. I'm so grateful for any work I can get."

"Well, I'll certainly let ya know if I have more. I do appreciate ya cleaning up in here once a week. The place fair sparkles when you're finished." He chuckled. "Shame that only lasts a short time and the men spoil all your hard work."

Aven fetched her shawl and threw it around her shoulders. "But if they didn't there'd be no need for me to clean and I really need the work. Perhaps I should thank the men for being slobs."

Whiskey Jim laughed out loud. "Yes, indeed, Miss Miller." He opened the cash register and took out a banknote. "Here you go."

Aven frowned. "A dollar? We agreed on seventy five cents."

"Well, ya did such a good job and ya fast and efficient. You deserve it."

Aven thrust her hands on her hips and scowled at him. "I don't want charity, Jim. I just want an honest wage for honest work."

"Alright." He smiled at her moxie. "As you wish." He opened the cash register again and slipped the dollar bill back inside, pulled out three quarters and passed them to her.

Aven smiled. "Much obliged, I'll see you next Wednesday morning."

Jim merely nodded and watched Aven march out. He folded his arms across his chest. Scoffing quietly, he shook his head. "That's a tenacious little lady. I respect her wanting to work hard." He nodded and looked around. "Still, a little charity never hurts now and then." He spoke out loud and reached for a glass from the spotless clean shelf.

Aven strode out the door and smiled. She pulled the reticule from beneath her dress and dropped her three quarters in. "That makes two dollars and fifty eight cents. More than halfway to paying off our debt at the store."

She strode into the store and up to counter. "Mr. Hansen." Aven called.

The man popped his head out of the storeroom. "I'll be right vif ya."

"Sure, I can wait." Aven strolled towards the shelves. She picked up the lilac soap, her favorite scent and sniffed it.

"Miss Miller," Mr. Hansen called.

Aven hurried to the counter.

"What can I do for you?"

Aven tipped out the contents of her reticule. "I want to put this on our account. I believe we owe three dollars and sixtyfive cents. I have two dollars fifty here and I'll use two dollars towards our debt and fifty cents to get eggs, flour, sugar and coffee, if it will stretch."

A slight twinkle entered Mr. Hansen's eye and Aven thought she saw the slightest smile. He stared intently at his ledger as he opened to the correct page. He raised his brows and looked up at her. "Your debt is only von dollar and fifty cents."

Aven frowned. "What do you mean? I was sure it was over three and a half dollars. And we owe you for the groceries last week."

"Then make it..." he counted up the amounts. "Two dollars, including vhat you vant today, then ve be even."

"That can't be right." Aven leaned over.

Mr. Hansen turned the ledger so she could see it. "There it is, the total." He thrust his finger at the amount.

"I don't understand."

The store man shrugged. "I don't know vhat to say, perhaps it was less than you thought?"

Aven shrugged. "Perhaps you're right. Well, that's an unexpected bonus. I'll have a little left over." She glanced up at the little doll again. *If only. But we still have a debt at the bank to pay off and this money would be better spent on new shoes for Amelia.* She sighed.

Mr. Hansen turned to look where she was looking. "Ya vant zee little doll?"

Aven shook her head. "I wish I could, I'd like to have it for my sister, but there are much more important things we need."

"Now ya account is paid, ya can take time off from vorking so hard."

"I'd like that, Mr. Hansen, but this isn't going to last long."

"I understand, Miss." He reached into the jar of gumdrops, scooped out a handful and put it into a paper bag. "Take zeese for ya sisters."

"I can't do that, Mr. Hansen. I don't have the spare money."

"It's a gift, really."

"You don't have to do that."

"I vant to, for zee little girl."

Aven swallowed her pride. "Thank you. You're very kind. The girls will be very excited."

"My pleasure, Miss."

Aven nodded and strolled outside. "Odd." She murmured to herself. "I could've sworn that debt was higher. And I've never known Mr. Hansen to be so generous." He'd given them a gumdrop or two from time to time, but a handful? That was unlike him.

"Another reason to be grateful, I guess." Aven shrugged. She glanced up at the clock on the bank and hastened her footsteps. Franky was expecting her at the livery in half an hour.

"Good day, Miss Miller." A cheerful voice stopped her in her tracks. She turned to see Austen leaning against an awning poll drinking his coffee.

She smiled. "Good day, Mr. Hart."

"You look happy."

"Oh, it's nothing really, I just had a spot of good fortune."

He raised his brows. "Oh?"

Aven smiled. "It just turned out my debt at the store was less than I remembered and for the first time since Papa died, we are in the positive with Mr. Hansen."

Austen nodded. "I'm glad. You deserve some good fortune."

"Thank you. Now if you'll excuse me, I have to get to the livery to help Franky. "

Austen frowned. "I hope you aren't overdoing it."

"Thank you for your concern, Mr. Hart, but I'll be just fine. I'm just doing what I must to take care of my family."

He nodded and smiled at her. "I understand, Miss Miller. I'm rather impressed by you."

Aven frowned. "Me?"

"Yes." Austen drained his cup and lay it on the horizontal rail. "I've never known a woman who's worked harder."

Aven screwed her mouth up. "Sometimes I wonder if I'm really a woman anymore. My hands are rough, my hair is all disheveled and I'm sure my face shows my tiredness."

Austen tilted his head to the side and eyed her up and down comically. "You certainly look like a woman to me. And a lovely one at that."

Aven chuckled. "I thank you, for the ego boost, Sir." She curtsied to him.

He tipped his head to her. "Miss."

Aven turned and headed for the livery. Austen leaned back against the post and smiled. *I'm glad such a small gesture has made her so happy. And not paying it all off means she's less likely to suspect it's me. I know how she feels about accepting charity.*

He felt the heat rise in his cheeks and his eyes lit up. *And I meant what I said, she's a very lovely woman. I'll do whatever I can to help her see that.* He picked up his coffee cup and headed back inside.

Ten

Aven followed her sisters into the pew and took a seat. She took a deep breath and exhaled, relishing the chance for a break. She closed her eyes and enjoyed the sound of the pianist warming up. It was her favorite hymn, Amazing Grace and she hummed along with the music.

"Is this seat taken?"

The voice startled Aven out of her meditative state and she jumped and opened her eyes abruptly.

"I'm sorry for frightening you, Miss."

"Oh, that's quite okay, Mr. Hart, I was enjoying the music." She smiled. "And no this seat isn't taken." She gestured to her sisters to move to the end of the row and she moved closer to Ada.

"Thank you." He smiled as he took his seat. "I don't know many people yet. I hope it's not inappropriate for me to sit here."

"Do you plan to do anything inappropriate?" Her eyes held humor.

Austen smiled. "Not unless singing hymns and reading my Bible is inappropriate." He lifted the black leather volume in the air.

"No, I believe that would be acceptable, Mr. Hart." She smiled and turned her head forward as the reverend stood to get their attention.

Austen tried to focus on the Reverend's words but his mind was distracted. This was the first time he'd ever seen Aven wear her hair long and in her best Sunday dress. Since it was the Sunday service she'd forgone the black mourning clothes and donned a pretty lavender gown she'd made herself.

Austen stole a glance at Aven as she closed her eyes to pray. She was really very beautiful and it was wonderful to see her so happy and relaxed, rather than harried and overwhelmed. *I wish there was a way I could make sure she remained this way forever.* The thought struck him out of the blue and he let out a small gasp.

Aven looked up at him quizzically. He nodded and smiled to let her know everything was just fine. She bowed her head again.

Austen's heartbeat sped up. Her proximity and the scent she wore sent thrills through him. *Pull yourself together, Austen. You're leaving town soon, you can't afford to fall for a woman.* He chided himself internally and forced his mind to focus on the Reverend's words. *Mind you, plans can change, can't they?*

* * * *

"Thank you for the meal, Mrs. Cartwright. It was most kind of you." Aven stood to help the woman clear the table.

The older woman smiled. "It's our pleasure. The reverend and I have been wanting to have you around for some time. You know times are tough for everyone in this town."

"Almost everyone." Ada scowled. "Mr. Mitchell could buy us all supper a hundred times over."

"But he wouldn't he's too mean," Amelia added.

Aven shot both her sisters warning glances to mind their manners and hurried to the kitchen behind Mrs. Cartwright. "We know only too well how tough times are. It was very kind of you to feed us. I'm sorry we have so little to contribute." She gestured to the half loaf of bread that remained. The only food she could manage to bring.

Mrs. Cartwright placed down the bowl she carried and turned to grip the younger woman's arm. "Don't worry about that, it's just the pleasure of your company that we want. We make do, the Lord provides for our needs."

"And ours." Aven nodded. "We aren't destitute yet." She attempted to sound lighthearted but she knew they barely had a day's worth of food at any time despite her working herself to the bone.

"He will provide for you. I'm praying for you all, cling to the Lord, Dear, and He'll see you through."

"Thank you. We will. Now we must get home. I have to cut enough wood to get us through the week," Aven said matter-of-factly.

Mrs. Cartwright meant to protest but she caught her husbands' eye. She merely nodded, they knew how independent Aven was. She wouldn't accept their charity even if they offered. "I understand."

Aven gave her a grateful smile, gestured to her sisters and they headed for the door.

"Ohh the wind is icy." Amelia pulled her coat tightly around herself and lifted the hood over her head.

"Yes. If we walk quickly, we'll keep warm. Now come on." Aven gripped the girl's hands and they hastened as fast as they could toward their home.

All three girls stepped to the side of the road as a horse and wagon approached.

"Well hello there," a brash voice called. Archie Mitchell pulled his horse to a halt and sneered at them.

Aven scowled and turned to keep walking.

Mitchell walked his horse alongside them. "Would you three like a ride?"

"No thanks, Mr. Mitchell, we are happy to walk." Aven tried to keep her voice polite.

"I won't bite, ya know. I'm just offering to take you home," he persisted.

Aven picked up the pace, suddenly wishing they weren't in such an isolated place. "I said, no thank you."

Archie growled. "Come on, I'm just offering you a ride. You are all in ya Sunday best, I'd hate to see you dirty up those pretty dresses walking in the dust and mud." He pretended to sound caring.

Amelia started to comment but Aven cut her off. "No, please, leave us be, Mr. Mitchell."

Archie sneered. "No one says no to me." He muttered. Pulling his horse to a halt he leapt off and gripped Aven by the shoulder yanking her around to face him. "I'm getting a little tired of you saying no to me."

Aven gestured to Ada to take Amelia and go home. Ada frowned her protest and Aven lifted her brows and pursed her lips. Ada got the point and gripped Amelia's hand and they ran in the direction of their home.

Aven looked Archie in the eye and squared her jaw. "And I'll keep saying no to you."

Archie frowned. "But you need me."

Aven raised her brows. "How so?"

"I'm rich, you have nothing, I need a pretty little wife,

and you need a wealthy benefactor to take care of those pretty little sisters of yours."

"No thank you, Mr. Mitchell, I'd rather starve than marry you."

Archie brought his face closer to hers. "I'm offering you a chance for a different life, you'll never struggle for money again if you marry me."

Aven frowned. "Why do you even want me?"

"You're the prettiest girl in this town, you're a hard little worker and...." He paused and eyed her up and down suggestively. "... and you have a good figure."

Aven shuddered visually. His gaze frightened her. "My answer is a definite and resolute no, Mr. Mitchell."

"Any woman would be glad to have me, I'm handsome, strong and rich... no one in their right mind would refuse me."

"Then I suggest you find one of those women." Aven turned to walk away.

Archie gripped her arm and leaned in to whisper in her ear. "I don't want one of those women. I want you, And I will have you. Mark my words."

Aven closed her eyes. "Let me go." She yanked her arm away from him and turned on her heels and ran away.

Archie scratched his chin as he watched her go. A sneer crossed his face. "I do like a woman with some spirit." He leapt up on his gig. "I will have her," he told his horse as he flicked the reins and headed towards his home.

*   *   *   *

Aven hurried up the stairs to her home. Pausing before she opened the door, she exhaled loudly. "Thank you, Lord that I got away from him. Give me courage and strength to know how to keep my family together."

She opened the door and walked in. "Hi girls." She smiled.

"Aven." Amelia ran over, she had already changed out of her church dress. She examined her older sister carefully, her dark eyes asking the question.

"I'm alright. I'd rather not speak about that man if you don't mind."

Amelia nodded and Ada gave her a relieved smile.

"I'll get changed and I'll be right out, I must get to wood chopping."

Amelia grinned. "You don't need to."

Aven frowned at her sister. "Of course I need to, we need firewood, Amelia."

"But you don't have to." Ada walked over to join the conversation. "It's already been done."

Aven's frown grew deeper. "What do you mean it's already been done."

"See for yourself." Ada pointed to the back door. "I went for the broom and I noticed it."

Aven opened the back door and stepped out onto the small covered porch. She looked across the back yard to the roughly constructed lean-to where she stored the firewood. She gasped and both hands flew to her mouth. "What on earth?" She stood wide-eyed staring at lean to with wood stacked in neat rows almost waist height. "That's enough wood to last us months."

"And then some." Ada grinned.

Amelia spun around to look at her sisters. "But where did this come from. Did you two arrange this?"

"No," both younger girls said simultaneously.

"Then who could it be?"

"We don't know. We thought maybe you'd bartered for the wood."

"No. I didn't, we have that fallen spruce over there that I've been cutting up."

"Well now you don't need to."

Aven smiled. "I guess not. I can't believe it. I wonder who could have done this."

"It doesn't matter does it? Someone is being kind to us."

"I suppose you're right." Aven shrugged. "Praise God for small mercies." She turned and followed her sisters back inside.

"So now you can rest for the afternoon, Aven." Amelia suggested.

"I have so much to do, I promised Mr. Clarke I'd help tidy the telegraph office, he has no clerk and the place is a mess. I'll go and do that job now, save me doing it tomorrow."

Ada thrust a cup of coffee in Aven's hand. "That job can wait. You are exhausted and need rest. Sit down and drink your coffee."

Aven meant to protest, she really ought to get to work, even if it was Sunday. But a wave of fatigue washed over her, and she slumped back into her seat. "I suppose I could take one afternoon off."

"Yay." Amelia ran to embrace her, narrowly missing spilling hot coffee all over them both as Aven quickly pulled the cup out of the way. "We miss you."

Aven smiled. "I miss you too, darling. It will be nice to take a rest."

"Yes, and later I can read to you. I'm getting real good now."

Aven smiled at Amelia. "I'm glad, you've struggled for so long, but your perseverance is paying off. I'd love to hear you read, after I finish my coffee and shut my eyes for a few moments."

Amelia nodded and hurried away to find her reader.

Eleven

Mr. Jensen looked up as Aven walked into the store. He observed her tired eyes and slouched figure. He gave her a sympathetic smile. The young woman was bone weary. He knew how hard she was working to feed her sisters.

Aven perused the shelves. She picked up a pretty haircomb and turned it over in her hands. It was lovely and it would suit Amelia. With a sigh she frowned and placed it back on the shelf. They barely had enough for the necessities without indulging in things they didn't need. She had saved just enough to buy the ingredients to make a cinnamon cake for the girl but there would be little else she could afford to celebrate. Amelia would have to be content with homemade gifts and a picnic by the river if it wasn't too cold.

Aven strolled to the counter and placed her basket down.

"Zis be all?" Mr. Jensen asked, reaching for the pencil he always kept tucked behind his ear.

"Yes, thank you." Her eyes lifted to the little doll above the counter again and she grimaced. "Yes, that will be all, thank you."

"It's ya sister's birsday tomorrow ain't it?"

"Yes."

"How are ya gonna celebrate?"

Aven sighed. She eyed the little doll again. "I'm afraid there isn't much we can do. I can't afford to buy her any gifts, but I have made her a new dress from one of Mama's old ones and we'll have cinnamon cake. It's her favorite."

"Zat sounds nice. Shame ya can't give ya sister a gift. She'd like zat pretty dolly."

"Oh, she'd love it, Mr. Jensen. But I just can't afford it. We can barely manage to get the essentials."

She looked up as Austen walked in. Squaring her shoulders she gave the man a determined nod, passed over her few coins and hurried out of the store. "Good day, Mr. Hart." She managed a resigned smile.

Austen grinned and briefly touched her arm as she walked past. "Good day, Miss Miller." He watched her leave and strolled to the counter. "I feel bad for her, she's on the brink of exhaustion."

The store man placed his pencil back in its customary location, nestled between the large soft tip of his ear and his straw-colored bristly hair. He leaned back against the shelf behind him and crossed his arms. "She vorks very hard to feed her family."

"Too hard if you ask me, if she's not careful she's going to collapse." Austen's voice held genuine compassion. "I wish there was a way I could help her."

"She's very proud, vouldn't even let me give her some free candy for her younger sister's birsday."

Austen nodded his understanding and scratched his chin. "When is her birthday?"

"Tomorrow, she'll be nine."

Austen frowned and leaned forward on the counter with his elbows. "I wish there was a way I could do something to help celebrate her birthday, to make it really special."

"You vould have to do it wisout her knowing, she'll not accept charity."

"I get it. I'll find a way." Austen exhaled and looked around. "What will I get? I don't know what to do for a child's birthday?"

Mr. Jensen smiled and raised his eyebrows, he reached up to the shelf above him and pulled down the little dolly. "She's had her eyes on zis for some time, but couldn't afford it."

Austen grinned and reached for the little doll. "It looks like the little girl."

"Yes, it does, only fifty cents."

Austen nodded and pulled a bank note from his pocket. He placed it on the counter. "Will this cover wrapping it, and putting a ribbon on it? Make it one that can be used for her hair as well."

"Yes, zat is more zan enough." The store man opened his cash register and slipped the note in. Lifting out some coins he held them out in his palm.

Austen shook his head. "The rest in candy, whichever is the girls favorite."

Mr. Jensen smiled and nodded. "Gumdrops!" he picked up a small paper bag and filled it with the sweets. "Zat be all?"

"I came in to see if you could mend my watch. I was told you were the one to come to."

"Let me see."

Austen pulled his pocket watch from his pocket and handed it to the older man. "It got wet and stopped working, I think there's water under the glass."

Mr. Jensen flicked it open and frowned. He ran his finger down the large crack in the glass. "Needs to be cleaned and new glass."

"Can you fix it? It was my grandfather's and it means a lot to me."

Jensen moved his mouth from side to side as he examined it in his large hands. "No, I don't zink I can, I can send it to ze city, zey have proper vatch makers there."

"Alright, please do that. I'd like to get it fixed."

"Won't be cheap, I'm afraid."

"How much?" Austen frowned.

"Maybe ten dollars."

Austen grimaced but nodded. "Alright. I'll get you the money. You send it away."

"Very good, Mr. Hart. I'll get zis in tomorrow's post. Probably take a few weeks."

"Much obliged." Austen picked up the wrapped doll and candy. "If you could keep this between us?"

The man nodded. "Of course."

"Thank you, good day."

*   *   *   *

"Shhh, you'll wake her up." Aven scolded her sister.

Ada frowned at her. "I'm being as quiet as I can." She fetched three plates from the high cupboard. "Have you finished with the cake?"

Aven grimaced and lifted it slightly for her sister to see. "This will have to do."

"It looks nice, you've done a great job."

"Thank you, it's the best I can do with what we have on hand. I used powdered sugar and this paper stencil I made." She lifted up the butterfly shape she'd cut from paper.

Ada smiled. "She'll love it, you've done a lovely job. You know she loves butterflies."

"Yes, I just wish I had something better to give her as a gift than this new dress I made." Aven sighed and closed her eyes. "She deserves so much better. I wish I could give her better."

"Hey." Ada placed the plates on the table and gripped Aven's arm. "She will love it, I promise. You don't have to feel bad, you work hard every day to make sure we have what we need and you go without. Amelia knows that."

Aven nodded and smiled at her sister. She turned to observe the table, their usual birthday pancakes sat in a pile with their last hoarded bottle of their mother's strawberry preserves. The cake sat right in the middle. "Something's missing."

"There is a small patch of late flowers around the side of the barn."

Aven smiled. "Go get some, I'll get a vase."

Ada nodded, thrust her coat on and opened the door. "What on earth?" She frowned and bent down to look at the package tied in brown paper and wrapped up with string.

"What is it?" Aven hurried over. "What on earth?" She echoed her sister's words. Leaning down, she scooped up the parcel and read the label attached. "Happy 9th Birthday, Miss Amelia."

Ada looked at her sister. "Who's it from?"

Aven turned over the tag. "It doesn't say."

"Maybe it's from the Reverend and Mrs. Cartwright." Ada guessed and closed the door as they stepped back inside.

"I suppose we'll never know, someone wanted to do something kind for Amelia. I wouldn't put it past the ladies of the town to do something nice. Mrs. Price has always had a soft spot for her."

Ada placed the parcel on the table and shrugged. "No matter who it's from, it means Amelia will get a surprise."

Aven sighed loudly and Ada gripped her arm. "I know what you're thinking but don't feel bad that you couldn't afford to do it, think of it as a blessing from the Lord because of your hard work. In a way it is from you."

Aven looked at her sister and gave her a kind smile. She embraced her. "Now we don't need the flowers. Come on, let's wake her up."

Amelia rubbed her eyes as she walked into the kitchen.

"Happy birthday, darling," both older sisters called and stepped aside to reveal the table.

Amelia's eyes lit up. "Wow." She smiled. "This is great. Thank you." She hugged Aven first then Ada. "Is it cinnamon cake?"

"Yes, of course." Aven pulled the chair out.

"What's that?" The little girl gestured to the package.

"It's a gift someone left for you."

Ada backed up her sister's words. "It was left here for you, we don't know who it's from."

Aven swallowed but managed a smile. "It's from God."

"Wow." Amelia pulled the gift close.

"Open it." Ada encouraged, while Aven stood by her.

Amelia pulled the string and let it fall onto the table. She carefully unfolded the paper, a useful commodity that could be reused. All eyes grew wide as she opened it to find the pretty little dolly from the store.

"Woooooow!" Amelia picked her up and tears flooded her eyes. "A real store-boughten doll."

Aven and Ada looked at each other.

"I wonder it if it was Mr. Jensen. He's the only one who knew I wanted to get the dolly for Amelia."

Ada grimaced. "Maybe, but maybe there was someone else in the store who heard? You never know."

Aven frowned. *It couldn't have been Mr. Hart, because he came in as I was leaving. Maybe there was someone else in the store.* She shrugged. "I guess we'll never know. Anyhow happy birthday sweet girl, I'm so glad you got your dolly, what are you going to name her?"

"Carolina."

Aven and Ada both squeezed their sister's shoulders. "Mama would be honored." Aven kissed Amelia's head.

"What's in that other package?" Ada pointed to a small brown paper bag.

Amelia put the doll carefully on her lap and lifted the small bag, she opened it and grinned. "Gumdrops!"

"Now that will be from Mr. Jensen. He tried to get me to take them earlier." Aven frowned. *I wonder why he did that? He must be responsible for the doll too.* She continued to mull over it as she dished pancakes onto each plate. *Mr. Jensen has always been a bit aloof but he's not an unkind man. Still, he's never seemed to be the charitable type, save for giving out candy now and again. Does this have anything to do with the firewood? Or is it all just a coincidence.* Aven shrugged and sparingly spread preserves on her pancake. *Oh well, I suppose whoever is doing these things doesn't want to be known. Mama always said to be grateful. Thank You Lord, for Your small blessings.*

* * * *

Austen nudged Princess into a gentle canter. "That's it, Girl. You're doing fine," he encouraged his equine companion. "That foot seems to have healed nicely." He slowed her to a walk and turned back to town, he didn't want to over do it on her first outing. He was glad she was finally healed. "So now what? Is California the place for me or should I stay..." A shriek brought an immediate halt to his introspective thoughts.

"Help me... Help me." The voice came from a nearby cabin.

Austen sprung into action. "Come on, girl." He hastened Princess towards the shrieks. A strange looking, rather scruffy horse stood out front with the most beat up old saddle he had ever seen. He could hear a scuffle happening in the cabin and muffled cries.

Without pulling Princess to a complete stop, he leapt off and burst through the door. A man had a young woman pinned against the kitchen wall at knifepoint with one hand over her mouth and his body pressed against hers. The terror in her eyes suggested the man's intentions were anything but honorable. He turned and glared at Austen.

"Take your hands off her." Austen strode towards them.

"Don't come no closer." He pushed the knife towards her neck, the point pierced her skin and blood began to flow down her slender neck onto her collar. "I'll do it, I really will."

Austen stopped walking "Alright. Put the knife down and we can discuss this."

"Ain't nothing to discuss, her papa owes me money, and I'm gonna get what I deserve one way or another." The intoxicated man sneered at the woman.

"Let her go." Austen looked around, he had to think fast.

"Or what?"

"Or I'll call the law." Was all Austen's feeble mind could come up with.

"There ain't no law in this town."

Before Austen could even think he snatched a piece of wood from the firebox and hurled it toward the man. He was too quick and ducked before it hit him, but it had the desired effect, the man dropped his knife and stepped away from the woman. She sunk to the floor and whimpered. Austen glanced at her, visually assessing her condition in a few seconds.

The man sprang to his feet but before he could reach for his knife Austen stepped on it. "You best leave, Mr."

"Or what?" The man was at least a head and shoulders taller than Austen and broad. He gripped Austen by the collar and slammed him against the wall. "I asked you a question, pipsqueak. What are you gonna do if I don't leave?"

Austen shuddered, the man's breath was a putrid mix of alcohol, tobacco and garlic. "Well for starters..." Austen lifted his knee and thrust it into the man's crotch.

"Ahhhh." He let Austen go and bent double. "What'd you do that for?" He squeezed between his teeth and collapsed to the floor.

Austen glanced at the woman, clutching her bleeding neck. "Are you alright?"

The woman gave him a nod and Austen turned as the man gritted his teeth. He threw a punch, but Austen ducked, and the man hit the milk pitcher which clattered to the ground and smashed into pieces. He gripped Austen in one hand and smacked him across the face, forcing his head back into the wall. Austen groaned and staggered to his feet, rubbing at his mouth as blood dripped from his lip. The older man threw another punch, forcing Austen to the floor, he sneered and reached down to grab him but something caught Austen's eye, he snatched up the discarded piece of firewood and conked the man over the back of his head. He collapsed, with his body falling over Austen. It knocked the wind out of him. He took a breath, pushed the unconscious man off himself and stood up, swiped at his mouth and hurried over to the woman.

He crouched before her, ignoring the pain in his own bruised jaw. "Are you alright, Miss?" He pulled out his handkerchief and held it to her. She flinched. "It's alright, Ma'am. I promise you'll be alright. Let me look at your neck?"

His caring eyes reassured her, and she nodded and moved her hand. Austen lifted his handkerchief to her neck and gently mopped up some of the blood so he could see the wound. "It's not too bad, nothing major is harmed, this area tends to bleed a lot, but you'll be okay. Hold this here and press firmly. I'll stitch you up." He looked around. "Do you have any sewing thread?"

The woman glanced nervously toward the man on the floor.

"He's out cold, we'll deal with him later, in the meantime we need to get that wound stitched up."

She nodded. "My sewing box," she whispered and pointed to a basket in the corner.

He gently touched her arm and hurried over to the basket, rummaging through, he found black thread, a needle and some scissors and he hurried back.

"Do you have any alcohol in the house?"

She gave him a quizzical look.

"To clean the wound."

She nodded and gestured to a high cupboard. He stepped over the unconscious man thrust open the cupboard and swiped a bottle of whiskey and the dishcloth hanging on a hook nearby. He crouched before her again and lifted her hand from her neck. He dabbed some alcohol on the cloth and wiped it at the wound. She winced.

"I think this is gonna need two stitches." His eyes held his sorrow to cause her pain.

She nodded.

"I'm sorry, Ma'am, I haven't got anything to give ya, I'm afraid it's gonna hurt. Here, take a mouthful of whiskey. It's not ideal but it may dull the pain a little."

She nodded again and took a mouthful, shuddering as the liquid hit her throat. "Do it."

He smiled. "I'll be quick.

Footsteps came up the walk. "Haley?" A man stood in the doorway and looked around. "What happened? Get away from my daughter!"

"Sir, I'm helping her, this man was hurting her." Austen gestured to the man.

The young woman's father calmed and nodded. He knelt and put his hand on his daughter's cheek. "Are you alright?"

"Yes, Papa. This man saved me."

"I was just about to stitch her wound, Sir. I have to get the bleeding stopped."

The man nodded and clutched her hand. As gently and quickly as he could Austen wove the needle in and out of her skin. She closed her eyes and gritted her teeth against the pain but didn't utter a sound.

"There, all done." Austen smiled. "You're a brave girl, Miss?"

"Turner." The man's eyes held grateful thanks.

"Miss Turner. You'll be fine. These stitches can come out in a week. Just be careful for a few days to not get them wet and don't move your neck too much if you can help it."

She gently turned toward him, grimacing as it stretched the stitches. "Thank you."

"Hart, the name's hart, Ma'am."

"Can I move her?"

Austen nodded and Mr. Turner scooped her up and carried her to the couch, sitting her down he threw a blanket over her. "You alright, darling?"

"Yes, Papa."

Mr. Turner cupped her cheek and leant down to kiss her forehead. "That's my brave girl."

She gave him a resigned smile.

Turner walked over to Austen who was watching the unconscious man carefully. He put his hand out. "What happened here?"

"I was riding past and I heard her screams, burst in and the man was hurting her. Had her at knifepoint. He cut her."

Mr. Turner swallowed and his brow furrowed deeply. He scowled at the man. "Edmonds!" He kicked out at the man; apart from a dull groan the man remained motionless. "It's about the money, aint it?"

"He said he would get what he deserves one way or the other. I believe he was planning to.... well... hurt her."

"I'm mighty grateful you came in when you did, I was in the back field, just came home for my noon meal and saw a strange horse."

"I'm glad too. I hate to think what might have happened to your daughter if I had been later."

Mr. Turner glanced across at Haley, she'd fallen asleep. He let out a deep breath. "Me too, and for you stitching her. Where'd you learn that?" He squinted at Austen.

Austen shrugged. "Something I picked up a while back, my father is a surgeon."

"Ahh, I see." The man nodded. "Well, let's get Edmonds out of here. He's a mad drunk."

"Let's get him to the livery, Franky'll have a chain we can lock him up with. Till we can get a sheriff here."

Mr. Turner nodded. "I'll get the wagon. Will ya stay here with Haley, I don't wanna leave her alone. I'll fetch Widda Price from cross the way to sit with her while we get this man outta my house."

Twelve

"Oh, please, let me help you with that." Austen hurried over and took the heavy full water pail from Aven's hands.

She began to protest but thought again and gave him an exhausted smile. "Thank you."

"Where were you going?"

"To empty it around the back of the saloon. Whiskey Jim won't let me do it out here, says it just makes mud and his customers drag into his saloon onto his polished floors. I don't know why it bothers him, when I'm the one who does the polishing." Aven managed a smile.

Austen nodded. "I'm happy to help." They fell into step together.

"I'm grateful."

"Are you finished for the day?"

"At this job, yes. I have two others to do before I go home to the girls."

Austen frowned. "You work too hard; don't you think you should take a break now and then?"

Aven stopped in her tracks and thrust her hands on her hips. "What choice do I have Mr. Hart? How do you suppose I'll keep the home fires burning and my sisters fed and clothed if I don't work?"

Austen placed down the pail and walked to her. "I understand, and of course you should work, but do you really need three jobs?"

"I'll take all the jobs I can get. No one wants to pay a woman much, and I need this money. As it is we live hand to mouth, never certain we'll have enough for the next day."

Austen closed his eyes. "I'm sorry. It's not fair is it?"

Aven squared her shoulders and lifted her chin. "Mr. Hart, I refuse to feel sorry. This is the situation we found ourselves in and we must do the best we can with the Lord's help to persevere through it."

"Still, it never hurts to take help from time to time."

"We don't need charity; we are just fine." She yawned and swiped her arm across her forehead.

Austen gently put a hand on her elbow. "Forgive me, Miss Miller, but you don't seem just fine. You seem like you're on the verge of exhaustion. If you don't slow down, you'll end up sick, then who's gonna take care of your sisters?"

Aven sighed loudly. "I wish I could take a break Mr. Hart, but I don't have a choice...." She grimaced. "There is one choice, but I'd rather gouge my eyes out with glass."

Austen raised his brows. "Oh?"

Aven shrugged. She wished she hadn't said anything. "Oh, there's just this rather persistent man who keeps trying to marry me. He's got money and tells me he's the answer to my problems."

"And he isn't?" Austen fought back the twangs of jealousy.

Aven shuddered. "No! I won't be unkind, but I wouldn't wish marriage to that man on anyone. His intentions don't seem entirely 'proper' if you get my meaning."

Austen worked very hard to keep the horror and anger from displaying on his face. *If I get my hands on him.* "Would you like me to speak to him for you?"

Aven shook her head and they continued walking. "No, I'm quite capable of refusing him. I don't even know why he wants to marry me. I know he doesn't love me."

"For some men it's about having a trophy, a pretty wife to make him look good and serve him. I'm glad you've got your wits about you, you'd be nothing but a slave and a whipping board to a man like that. He sounds very unpleasant."

"He makes my skin crawl."

"Well, you won't have to marry him. I promise you that."

"I have no intention of ever marrying him, no matter how much he asks, or you promise." She squinted at him. "Why do you care anyway?"

"I just don't wanna see anyone get hurt, least of all my friends."

"Are we friends, Mr. Hart?"

Austen strode to the corner of the lot and upended the pail onto the grass. He turned back and grinned at her. "I hope we might be. Don't you?"

Aven gave him a genuine smile. "Yes, I'd like that. Thank you." She put a hand out for her pail.

"I'll carry it back to the saloon for you, give you a few minutes break before your next job."

"Much obliged, good sir."

He dared reach an elbow out to her. She chuckled and slipped her arm under his. "Much obliged." She shuddered as they rounded the corner toward town and a cold wind hit her.

"It's getting chilly."

"Yes, I expect it'll snow soon." Aven's face lit up. "I love snow."

"I can tell by your eyes."

"Of course that's going to make finding work much harder. I hope to save enough to get us through the winter. Ada helped me do extra canning this year so we aren't quite destitute yet, barring an emergency." She whispered the last part as though saying it aloud might make it happen.

"You'll be just fine. So, what is it you love about snow?" He smiled as they reached the saloon.

Aven smiled back at him. "I don't know, the whole world gets covered in this blanket of white, like it gets to start again, fresh, unblemished and pure. There's something magical about it for me."

Austen grinned. She was growing more and more wonderful in his mind. It was getting harder and harder to think about leaving this place and her. "What do you like to do in the winter?" He didn't know why he was asking these questions. He just couldn't help it; she was so interesting and strong.

"Well..." She bit her lips together. "I love to skate and..."

He squinted at her. "And?"

"You'll think me silly." She hung her head. "And childish."

Austen smiled, and gently lifted her chin so he could look her in the eye. "You are not silly or childish, you could never seem that way to me."

The intensity of his gaze made her blush. "Well, as long as you promise you won't laugh, I'll tell you."

He leaned his head in and fixed his eyes on hers. "I wouldn't laugh at you."

"Very well, I'd... well... I'd love to ride in a sleigh, decorated with ribbons and drawn by two white horses."

Austen gave her a wide smile and nodded. "A sleigh?"

"You promised you wouldn't make fun."

"I'm not making fun of you. I think that's a wonderful dream. Have you never ridden in a sleigh before."

"Sure, I have, once or twice but not a fancy storebought sleigh all decorated for Christmas. Many years ago, a wealthy woman came to town on Christmas Day in a beautiful sleigh and I've always dreamed of being carted away in one by the..." She stopped herself and bit her top lip. Her cheeks colored deeply. "Nevermind."

"By the?" She had him captivated, the way her face lit up and her eyes sparkled over such a simple wish.

"Well by the man I love. I always kinda dreamed about having a winter wedding and driving away..." Her voice petered out.

"In a decorated sleigh drawn by two white horses." He smiled. *I would love to make that dream come true for her.* The voice deep in his spirit made him inhale sharply.

"See, it's silly."

"Miss Miller, it's not silly, sometimes it's the simplest dreams that make us the happiest."

Aven tipped her head to the side. "What about you?"

"What about me?"

"I've told you my simple dream, what about you?"

"I have many dreams, but there is one thing I always wanted to do."

Aven raised her brows.

"I've always wanted to be a good skater."

Aven's face dropped. "You don't know how?"

Austen shrugged. "I've attempted one or two times but there was never much need in the city."

"No, I suppose not."

"Do you skate, Miss Miller?"

"Of course, when I was a girl we used to have skating parties all the time. We even had an ice-ball one year."

"An ice-ball, I've never heard of that."

Aven smiled. "That's 'cause we made it up."

"What is an ice-ball?"

"We got all dressed up in gowns and suits, warm woolen coats. We decorated up Whisker Lake which was frozen solid. We had food and drinks for sale and a band played, and we skated and danced together in the lamplight. It was wonderful." Aven clasped her hands together.

A wide slow smile crossed Austen's face. "That does sound wonderful."

Aven scowled. "Now, don't tease, I know we're little better than provincials to city boys like you, but here that might as well have been a city cotillion."

"I'm not teasing...." Austen's words were stolen by the clock on the post office.

"Oh." Aven gasped loudly. "I'm late. You've distracted me with all this chitchat, Mr. Hart. I better return Whiskey Jim's pail and get to the livery."

Austen snatched the pail away from her outstretched arm, holding it behind him. "I'll return the pail, you get to work."

Aven frowned and scowled at him. "You'll keep."

"I hope so." He winked at her.

Aven shook her head and hurried away.

Austen stood and watched her go. "An ice ball." He grinned and his eyes widened. "A horse-drawn sleigh!" He nodded and scratched his chin. "I believe that could be arranged," he murmured and strolled into the saloon to return the pail.

"Say, Mr. Hart?" a voice called as he stepped back outside.

Austen spun on his heels to see where the voice had come from. The man wore a tin star pinned to his lapel. "Sheriff? What can I do for you?" He put his hand out to the man.

The sheriff took the hand and shook. "O'Reilly."

"Hart, Austen Hart."

"Yes, I know who you are."

Austen squinted at him.

"Mr. Barnes, the Mayor, pointed you out to me."

Austen nodded and waited for the man to continue.

"You're probably aware that we've arrested Mr. Edmonds and I've got him loaded up to take back to Cloudy Ridge with me." He gestured toward the jail wagon across the street with a deputy sitting in the seat.

Austen nodded again and scratched at his chin. "I'm glad. He's a very evil man, he thought nothing of hurting a young lady."

"I heard. And I heard you saved her life."

"I'm not sure about that, I was just doing what I could."

"It sounds like you are just the man the town needs."

Austen frowned. "Me, Sir?"

"Yes, the mayor and I were wondering if you'd take on the tin star?"

Austen's eyes widened and his mouth dropped. "Excuse me, Sir, are you asking me to be sheriff."

"That's exactly what I'm asking. You seem to me to be man of excellent character, plenty brave and you took down a man a lot bigger than yourself."

"Um... well... I'm not sure I'm big or strong enough."

"Size and strength have nothing to do with it. You have cunning and wisdom and compassion. All valuable to a smart sheriff. The mayor agrees with me, you're the right man."

Austen scratched his chin. "I'm not sure I'm the right man, but if you think I could do it, I could try. I don't know enough about the law, though."

"That's where I come in. You'd come to me for a time, fill in as a deputy for say a month or so, learn the ropes and then come back and you can take up the job here."

Suddenly the thought of being away from Aven and the town was awful. He paused and took a deep breath. "I'd like to think about it, if you don't mind. When would you need to know?"

"I was hoping you'd come back with me."

"Oh, that's too soon, I'd have to tie up some loose ends and..."

The sheriff frowned. "The mayor told me you were unattached."

"I... that is I am. But I do have responsibilities keeping me here."

"I thought you hadn't found a job yet."

"Well, yes, that's true but..." He could think of no valid reason to refuse, except for watching over Aven. "I'm not sure I can be away from town for so long."

"What's keeping you here?"

"Ah, well.... Ah... Nothing... Really."

The sheriff squinted at him then nodded and smirked. "A girl?"

Austen smiled without meaning to. "Ah, something like that, Sir."

The sheriff crossed his arms over his chest. "It's not forever, Mr. Hart. You can come back to her."

"I know that, it's just, she's having a hard time of it at the moment and I kinda hoped to be around to well... kinda... keep an eye on things."

"You could come and go occasionally to check up on your girl, if that makes you feel better. It's a half day's hard ride there and back, provided the snow isn't too heavy."

Austen nodded. "Alright. I'll do it, on one condition. That I can start Monday, give me time to make some arrangements here." He scratched his chin again. "And she isn't my girl..."

"She isn't?"

Austen gave him a sideways grin. "Leastways, not yet."

The sheriff gave him a knowing smile. "I understand. If you do take on this job, young man, you'll have to make sure your head is in the game."

"It will be."

The Sheriff nodded. "Alright. I'll see you at my office in Cloudy Ridge on Monday morning."

"I'll be there, Sir."

Thirteen

"Thank you for bringing me home, Mr. Packard" Aven gave the man a tired smile.

"You're welcome, Miss Miller. Your cabin is on my way home anyway."

"I appreciate it, and the work."

He nodded as he helped her down from the wagon. "My pleasure, you're a hard worker. I'll give you that."

Aven nodded and walked toward the house as Mr. Packard climbed back up onto the wagon and flicked the rein.

"Oh, Mr. Packard?" Aven turned.

The man pulled the confused horse to a stop and looked at her.

Aven gave him a hopeful smile. "Should there be any other work..."

The man grimaced. "I'm sorry, Miss Miller, Tommy'll be back at work tomorrow." He shrugged. "I really am sorry."

"I'll do anything, clean your office, wash the windows, even cook for you?" Her eyes pleaded with him.

"I'll give it some thought, Miss Miller. I wish I could make you promises but... you see... I can barely afford to keep Tommy employed." He grimaced.

Aven's face dropped. "I understand. Thank you."

He nodded, clucked to the horse and walked away.

Aven took a deep breath and exhaled loudly. She remembered her father's words. "Breathe out all your troubles before you walk in the door, then you don't burden your family with them." She chuckled and breathed out again, to make sure she got them all out. "I wish I could breathe out and take away the exhaustion too...." Aven frowned as something caught her eye, putting down her basket, she peered behind the small shrub off to the side of the porch. "What on earth?" She stepped back down off the porch and walked over to take a look. It was a large wooden crate with the lid nailed on. Aven frowned and bent down to look at it. Painted on the top was 'Miller family.' "What on earth?" she said again.

Aven picked up the box, with a loud groan, she could only barely lift it, managing with great difficulty to stagger up the stairs and bang on the door.

Ada opened it. "Aven?" She looked at her sister. "What's that box?"

"I don't know but if you could step aside so I can put this down, it's really heavy." Aven hissed out between her gritted teeth.

"Oh, sorry." Ada chuckled and stood aside to let Aven in, then snatched the basket from the porch and followed her sister inside.

Amelia walked over. "What's that?" She pointed to the table where Aven placed the box.

Aven shrugged. "I dunno. It was sitting behind the yew bush."

Ada frowned. "We've been home all day; we didn't hear anything."

Aven shrugged. "Well, someone put it there and it has our name on it." She pointed to the painted words.

"Let's open it." Amelia grinned.

Aven nodded. "Ada, fetch me a hammer."

Ada hurried to the back porch and fetched her father's hammer. "Here you go."

It took some time but eventually Aven had the lid pried off. She laid it aside and all three girls faces lit up and they looked at each other in surprise. The box was full of pantry staples, vegetables, eggs and a few mystery packages wrapped in brown paper and tied up with string.

Aven put her hands to her face. "I wonder who this is from?"

Ada and Amelia shrugged. "I don't know, but this is enough food to last us a few weeks!" Ada exclaimed.

"We'll eat like queens." Amelia's eyes lit up.

"What's in the parcels?" Ada lifted one out.

"Open it and see." Aven nodded.

"Wow." Amelia grinned as she opened the parcel. "Beefsteak, chicken, even ham, enough to last us a week."

"Amelia, open this one." Aven passed a large soft parcel to her youngest sister.

Amelia placed it on the table and loosened the string on the package. "Wow!!" she exclaimed and lifted up a brand-new pair of stockings. There were three of those, ribbons, even some yardgoods. "Hey there's a card."

Aven snatched it up before the others could move. She read aloud.

"A small blessing, from a friend."

Aven turned the card over. "There's no name on it."

"Maybe one of us has a secret admirer." Amelia swooned. "After all its not the first strange thing that's happened."

"Don't be silly, it's likely someone feels sorry for us and wanted to do something kind." Ada smiled.

Aven chewed on her lower lip, her telltale sign when something perplexed her.

Amelia frowned. "What is it?"

"You don't suppose it was Mr. Mitchell?" Aven grimaced.

"I doubt it, that man doesn't have a kind bone in his body." Ada scowled. "He'd never think of someone else, let alone care about things ladies need." She gestured to the package, Amelia lifted up some linen fabric, ideal for underthings.

"But who else in this town would have enough money for all this"

"Ohhhh." Amelia thrust a hand over her mouth. There were three bars of fragrant soap and a bottle of scent.

"Ohhh." Aven brushed a tear. "Who did all this? We can't accept all this."

Amelia frowned at her "Why not?"

"Because we didn't earn it."

Ada gripped her sister's arm. "Remember what Ma and Pa used to say. Never be surprised when God blesses you, just be grateful."

"But it's charity." Aven's voice sounded less convinced.

"Aven, Papa used to say we should help those in need, whenever we could. So why shouldn't we let someone help us. We sure could use these things." Tears flooded the little girl's eyes. "Then you won't have to work so hard and be gone all the time." She lowered her head. "I miss you."

Aven put an arm around Amelia and nodded. "You're right as usual, darling. Of course we would help another family if we could."

Amelia threw her arms around her sister. "This is so wonderful. I think we should thank Jesus."

Aven squeezed her sister. "Yes, we absolutely should." Her voice chocked a little. "We absolutely should."

The three sisters sat down, held hands and Aven's voice trembled as she prayed a grateful prayer for His provision. They looked up at each other and grateful tears filled all eyes.

Aven squeezed both girl's hands. "Well, we better get these things packed away."

"I want beefsteak for supper." Amelia grinned.

Aven smiled. "I'll just go and wash up and then we'll get started on supper."

Ada lifted out a bag of flour. "We'll start on supper."

Amelia lifted out the small bag of potatoes and licked her lips. "Potatoes are my favourite."

"Use them sparingly girls, we have to make this last." Aven smiled.

"We will, you go take a bath, we have the water heating."

* * * *

It was a small gesture comparatively, but it made Austen happy to know they were cared for while he was gone. He'd arranged for Mr. Jensen to have another crate delivered in two weeks time and if he was still away, the following week. The snow would be heavy on the ground by then and it would make life even tougher for them. "Well, when I get back I'll see to it they get through winter safe and sound. Maybe even a few special treats." He grinned as he walked upstairs to his room in the boarding house. "Perhaps an ice-ball?" He chuckled as he thought about skating hand in hand with Aven, both gliding over the lake.

"Lord, watch over Aven and her sisters while I'm gone." The thought of leaving caused his heart to ache. "And keep her safe." He would use the time away to make sense of his feelings. He hoped he could pluck up the courage to tell her how he felt before he left.

It wasn't until Sunday that he got a chance to be alone with Aven. After the service he hurried out to meet her on the stairs. "Miss Miller, I wondered if you might take a brief walk with me?"

Aven gave him a quizzical look. "A walk?"

"There's ahhh... something I want to talk to you about."

Aven raised her brows. "oh?"

"Will you walk with me, just across to the oak, in full sight of everyone, I promise, I'll be brief."

"Well..." Aven glanced up at her sisters. "The girls have been invited to dine with the Bradleys, I was going to get a head start on my sewing but I can catch up later."

"Is that yes?" Austen smiled

Aven returned his smile and nodded. "As long as it's brief."

Austen nodded and held his elbow out to her.

She chuckled and slipped her hand in his. He smiled, enjoying the warmth of her so close to him. Struggling to work out how to steer the conversation to what he really wanted to say, he blurted out the first thing he could think of. "Are you cold?"

"No, this thick coat is really warm."

"It looks it, with all the fur in the lining."

"Papa caught a bear going after our sheep a few years back, he killed it and the whole town ate for a week. We used the fur to make coats for the whole family."

Austen crinkled his nose. "You ate bear?"

Aven smiled. "Yes, it's not my favorite meat, but it was tasty as a stew and when you're hungry you'll eat most anything."

Austen nodded, he'd never known what it was like to wonder where his next meal would come from. He swallowed the lump in his throat and wished he wasn't leaving. He still couldn't bring himself to get to the point. They walked in silence enjoying the crunching of the snow below their feet.

Aven sighed and looked around.

"Everything alright?" Austen's eyes examined her.

"Yes." She smiled. "I just love new snow, isn't it beautiful?"

He grinned back at her. "Yes, it is beautiful." He caught himself before he added *But not nearly as beautiful as you are in that dress and fur coat.* The smell of her perfume made his heart lurch. He recognized it as the perfume he'd chosen at the store. When Mr. Jensen wasn't looking he'd sprayed it on his handkerchief. Now he took it out when he needed to and smelled it and it made him think of her. He blushed slightly as he thought of his foolishness. He hoped that smell would last long into his trip away.

"Well, we're at the oak." Aven let go his arm and shrugged.

"Take a seat." He gestured to the snow-covered long bench that had been placed with a view over the common and the frozen lake. "Oh." He laughed at her horrified look. He leaned down and pushed the snow off the chair, unbuttoned his coat and lay it down."

"But you'll be cold?" She questioned him.

"I don't care. Please, sit." He gestured. *I'd strip down to my bare chest to see that you are comfortable.* He didn't know where these thoughts were coming from.

"Okay." She smiled. Aven took a deep breath; her heart rate began to rise as he sat next to her on the small stool. His proximity made her gasp inadvertently. She dragged those thoughts in line by concentrating on the conversation. "So, what did you want to say?"

Austen took a deep breath and pulled the tin star from his pocket and showed her.

Aven frowned. "I don't understand."

"I've been asked to be the sheriff."

Aven's brows flew up and her mouth fell open. "What do you mean?"

"I mean, I'm going to be sheriff. They heard about me saving Miss Turner's life and they've asked me to be the sheriff."

Aven's lip trembled, she bit it to stop it giving away her fear.

Austen examined her face. "What is it."

"It's so dangerous."

"I'm not going to take unnecessary risks. But someone needs to protect you... the town and make sure people are safe."

"I suppose so. Please promise me you'll be careful."

Austen's heart skipped a beat, it thrilled him she cared so much about him. "I will of course."

"So is that what you wanted to tell me?" She creased up her brows.

"Yes, I wanted to tell you I'm going to be sheriff and... well... I'm going to be out of town for a while."

The lurch in her heart caught Aven by surprise. "You are?" She tried to keep her emotions from her face.

"Yes, the sheriff over at Cloudy Ridge is going to make me his deputy for a while so I can learn the job and the law."

Aven nodded. "How long will you be gone?"

"A month, give or take."

Aven took a deep breath and exhaled. "Alright." She examined her hands in her lap, and both sat in silence. After a time, Aven looked up at him. "Mr. Hart?"

Austen fixed his eyes on hers. "Austen, please."

She smiled. "Austen?"

"Yes?"

"Why did you feel like you needed to bring me here to tell me this?"

Austen managed a shaky smile as he scrambled for a good excuse. "Well... uh... because we're friends and I didn't want you to find out from anyone else."

"Why?"

"Because I care about you." Austen tried to keep his voice casual.

Aven smiled. "Take care of yourself. I'll see you in a month or so." Her voice sounded calm but internally she was weeping. *Please don't go.* Her eyes pleaded. "Is that all?" She had to change the subject before she burst into tears.

"Yes. I just wanted you to know. I will be back, I promise."

"I know." She stood. "I need to get to my sewing."

Austen stood and gave her his arm again. "I'll walk you home."

"There's no need, I can walk."

"I know you can. I'd like to."

"Alright." She smiled. Her heartbeat pounded in her ears. Was he saying he had feelings for her? Was he just being a considerate friend? She was more confused than ever.

They walked slowly through the snow and made small talk. After a time they fell into a comfortable silence until they reached her home. They walked up onto the porch and Aven heard herself say, "Would you like to come in for some coffee? The girls will be home by now."

Austen smiled. "I'd like that, very much."

He opened the door and held it for her while she walked in. The two younger girls had both changed and were seated in the lounge reading. Amelia had her doll on her lap as she usually did.

"Hi girls. You remember Mr. Hart." Aven's cheeks reddened without her realizing it.

Ada looked at Amelia and both smiled. They turned back to him and stood up. "Yes, hello Mr. Hart."

Aven looked at Ada. "He's Sheriff Hart now." She smiled, a sense of pride and fear washed over her.

Austen frowned. "I'm just Austen, please. You don't need to be so formal."

"It's polite. Sheriff." Amelia smiled and placed her doll on the chair.

"Hey, that's a pretty dolly." Austen smiled, hoping to keep the secret well hidden.

Amelia grinned and picked her up, bringing her over to him. He took the doll from her and gave her a thorough examination. "She's very pretty, she looks a lot like you." He cupped the little girls cheek. "Same blue eyes and pretty brown curls."

Amelia beamed. "Her name is Carolina."

Austen smiled and passed the doll back to the girl. "That's a pretty name."

Aven nodded. "It was our mother's name." She glanced up at the portraits over the fire.

Austen followed her gaze. "She was a beautiful woman. You know you look a lot like her."

Aven blushed. "Thank you. I'll get you some coffee." She gestured to the couch and hurried to the kitchen to get control of her emotions.

* * * *

Austen strolled into the boarding house with his hands in his pockets and a grin on his face. He sighed. There was no doubt in his mind now that he was falling for Aven Miller. She was a tenacious and brave young woman with so much strength and integrity. To top it all she was beautiful. He dared to let himself dream of a future with her. *No, pull yourself together, you'll be apart for more than a month. Use that time to make yourself worthy of her.* His thoughts were interrupted by a cry from the room off the kitchen. He could hear Mrs. Grant trying to soothe her. He frowned. That was Mrs. Watson's room. *She must be in labor.* He grimaced as she cried out again. Those weren't the usual cries of labor. He recognized a woman in distress. He took two steps towards the stairs up to his room and stopped as a phrase entered his mind. 'First do no harm.' It was his medical school oath. He closed his eyes and exhaled loudly.

Taking a deep breathe he walked to the door and knocked loudly.

"Just a minute." He heard a shuffling and the sound of a woman whimpering. Mrs. Grant opened the door. "Oh, Mr. Hart, this isn't a good time." She gestured to the bedroom. "Mrs. Watson is in labor."

"I know, and in distress." His face full of compassion and worry.

Mrs. Grant frowned but merely nodded.

"I can help."

"It's okay, Son. I'm a midwife." She sighed and rubbed her cheek. "But I ain't never seen this before." Her voice was low and raspy and Austen noticed her shudder as another cry echoed through the halls.

"What's the matter?"

"I don't rightly know. She been hurting for most of the day, and he don't seem no closer to coming."

"Let me help?"

Mrs. Grant raised her brows.

"Please, trust me Mrs. Grant. I've seen this before." She frowned at him.

"My father is a surgeon and a GP. I've been around medicine for years."

The woman grimaced as Mrs. Watson cried out again. What choice did she have? "Alright."

He nodded. "I'll go wash up. Get her prepared for me to examine?" He desperately hoped he didn't sound too much like a doctor.

Mrs. Grant nodded and hurried back to the woman.

Soon Austen was back, he'd removed his coat and rolled up his sleeves. Mrs. Grant could see he'd washed his face and arms and hands thoroughly they were almost red from scrubbing. He walked to her bedside. "Mrs. Watson, I'm a do..." he sighed and caught Mrs. Grant's narrowing eyes. He bit his lip and begun again. "That is, I've got some experience in delivering babies. I'm going to see what's happening, alright."

Mrs. Watson looked worried and groaned as a pain shot through her.

"Trust him, he knows what he's doing." Mrs. Grant smiled and patted the younger woman's hand.

Mrs. Watson nodded.

Austen examined her and grimaced. "Mrs. Grant, might I have a word?" He wiped his hand on a towel and walked to the corner of the room and the woman followed.

"What is it, Mr. Hart, have you seen this before?"

"Yes I... that is, I helped my father with a birth like this some time ago."

"What is it?"

"The baby is backwards and twisted up."

"Breach?"

"Yes, exactly."

"What can be done?"

"My father had to turn the baby around, it's very painful and risky but it's the only chance of saving the mother and baby."

"Can you do it?"

"Yes, I think I can. But it's going to hurt, a lot."

"She's brave, she'll manage."

"I'll need your help, Ma'am. If you're up to it?"

"Just tell me what to do."

"Can you explain to her what needs to happen? I advise you to wrap two strips of sheet around the bars at the end for her to pull on. She'll need them to help when she has to push." He spoke in a low voice, between the cries of the woman on the bed.

He gave her an urgent look and she nodded and hurried away to oblige. Austen walked back to Mrs. Watson. "Ma'am, your baby is in a difficult position."

"Will he.... Ahhhhhhh. Will he be... okay?" she managed.

"I believe so, but I'm afraid it's going to be a lot more painful than it normally would be. I'm sorry." He gripped her shoulder briefly.

She nodded.

He gave her a smile and positioned himself for the birth. Mrs. Grant walked in and placed the basin of hot water and a towel on the small table. He nodded his thanks and gestured for her to take her place alongside the woman.

"Now, Mrs. Watson, I'm going to have to turn the baby around. I'm afraid this is going to hurt, a lot and it won't be a quick procedure."

Mrs. Grant wiped the woman's brow with a cool cloth. "Do you understand?"

"Yes." Mrs. Watson nodded and called out again.

"I suggest you grit your teeth." He placed his hands on her stomach, either side of the baby. "I'll go as quickly as I can."

Mrs. Watson took a deep breath and gritted her teeth. She cried out as Austen with gentle pressure turned the baby. He paused and let her catch her breath. "Just a little more." He encouraged. "Take another breath."

She inhaled and screamed as he repositioned his hands and forced the baby around until his head was in the right place. "All right, that's the worst of it. I promise." He swiped his hand across his brow. "Take a rest for a moment, soon it'll be time to push..."

Austen stepped out of the room with Mrs. Grant on his heels. "Praise the Lord they both made it." He sighed.

"Yes, and she's sleeping at last. I'm glad she's got a boy to remember her James by."

Austen nodded. "Yes." He folded his arms over his chest and leaned against the wall. "He's quite a little chap." What was that longing in his heart? Was he yearning for a family of his own?

"How did you know what to do, Mr. Hart?"

"I told you; my Father is a surgeon."

"Yes, my father was a carpenter but none of my brothers know his trade." She raised her brows and gave him a knowing look.

"Please don't say anything, Mrs. Grant." He kept his voice low.

"I won't, but I don't understand why you want to keep it to yourself. This town could use your skills."

"Please, Mrs. Grant. It's a part of my past I'd rather not relive." His loud sigh and shudder made Mrs. Grant bite back her retorts.

She nodded and gripped his arm. "Your secret is safe with me, Mr. Hart. But I hope you change your mind one day."

He shook his head. "I can't." He stood up straight and turned to move. "I'll check on her before I leave in the morning."

Mrs. Grant nodded. "I'll stay with her. Goodnight Mr. Hart."

"Goodnight. Mrs. Grant."

* * * *

Austen nudged Princess into a lilting canter and headed up the north road. He had half a day's hard ride ahead of him and he spent most of it thinking and praying. He thought back over the previous day, his conversation with Aven and their growing friendship, and Mrs. Watson and her baby. Mrs. Grant had worked out that he was a doctor. "So much for keeping that secret." He sighed. But there was no way he could have walked away from the woman. He was certain that without his help she and the baby would have died. Mrs. Grant had asked him why he didn't want anyone to know he was a doctor.

He knew the reason, he was afraid. Afraid to face his past and have others depend on him again. Mrs.

Watson had survived but what about his next patient, or the next? Sooner or later, he'd lose another one. "I just can't do it." He shook his head. "So. I'll be sheriff." He chuckled. "How'd I ever end up sheriff?"

He turned his thoughts to Aven. The further he got from her the more his heart ached. He shook his head again. "You're long gone." He laughed at himself. "But what will she do when she finds out my secret? Will she ever trust me?" he sighed. "Lord, help me to work out where You want me. Help me to work out who you want me to be and where, if any, Aven fits into all this."

Fourteen

Aven wandered through the snow in the early hours. The sun was just peeking over the horizon and, there was just enough light to see the familiar path. She pulled her fur coat tighter around her shoulders. She smiled as she thought about how Austen had admired her coat. She was surprised at how much she missed him. She hadn't known him long but she was drawn to him, felt safe and comfortable and protected with him. But it was more than that. She hunted in her mind for the word. A bright smile crossed her face. "Cherished," she whispered. "I feel cherished by him."

She chuckled and shook her head at her own sentimentality. He'd done nothing overt to win that praise; it was in his mannerisms, his kindness, the gentleness of his touches, the way he looked at her. She took a deep breath and sucked back the feelings. "Don't get ahead of yourself, Aven, you have no reason to believe he has feelings for you at all. Besides, I'm not sure I could court now that he's sheriff, I'd constantly be afraid."

Still, he was so different from Archie Mitchell. The older man was absolutely persistent. In the week that Austen had been away Archie had doubled his efforts. It seemed there was hardly a day that went by that she wasn't propositioned by him. He was getting more aggressive too. He'd done nothing to physically hurt her but she didn't know what he was capable of. She dare not let him near her sisters. She shuddered and deliberately pushed any thought of the vile man from her mind and concentrated instead on the job before her. She pushed open the saloon door that Whiskey Jim left open for her and closed it behind her. Keeping her thoughts desperately in submission she focused with all her might on the task before her.

*   *   *   *

Ada looked up from her mending and frowned at the door. "Who would be calling at this time?"

Amelia jumped up from her chair. "I'll get it."

Ada grimaced. *Any excuse to get out of studying history.* She shook her head and chuckled, turning her head back to the stocking she was repairing. Hearing Amelia gasp she snapped her head up.

"Mr. Mitchell. What are you doing here?" Ada shuddered, stood and strode over to put her hand on her sister's shoulder and pull her back slightly from the man.

Archie noticed the gesture and scowled. "Where's your sister?" There was a sinister look in his eye that Ada didn't like.

"She's at the...?"

"I don't know...." The two girls spoke at the same time. Ada gave Amelia a stern glare and gestured with her eyes to stop. She turned to look at Archie. "She's out working, I'm not sure where today," she lied, giving an exaggerated shrug. She hoped that would be enough to get him to go away.

He squinted at her and screwed up his face. He looked from Ada's face to Amelia's. "I think you're lying to me. You do know where she is."

Ada was about to lie again when Archie thrust a hand out and yanked Amelia towards him. The girl let out a whimper and fixed scared eyes on her sister. Archie put one arm around her waist and lifted her off her feet. She shrieked and flailed her arms around. "Stop that squirming or I'll give you a reason to squirm." His voice was so menacing that Amelia froze in terror, still looking at her sister.

Archie sneered at Ada. "You will tell me where Aven is or I'll take this one instead." He made a dramatic scene of sniffing her hair and smirked. "She smells so sweet."

"Put my sister down." Ada lunged forward to try to pull the younger girl from his arms.

Archie moved out of her reach. "I will when you tell me where Aven is." He sniffed the girls neck that time and Ada noticed Amelia shudder.

"She's working." Ada blurted out.

Archie squinted at her. "She's working where? I just came from the saloon and the bar keeper said she finished up there at six am and hurried out to a job but he wouldn't tell me what it was."

"Why should I tell you?" Ada folded her arms over her chest and gave him a defiant look.

Archie bent down without loosening his grip on Amelia. He brought his face close to Ada's. "Because you don't want to know what I'll do if I don't find out?"

Ada squinted at him. "What do you want her for?"

Archie smirked. "Ain't none of your business."

Ada thrust her hands on her hips. "Then it ain't none of your business where she is."

Archie squeezed Amelia tightly and a low groan came from his throat. He pushed the girl from him onto the couch and growled. "You'll be sorry you messed with me. I will find Aven, and she'll be my wife, you'll see." He turned and stomped out the door.

Amelia stood and ran to Ada and the two girls embraced. "Are you alright?"

Amelia nodded and stepped out of the embrace. "What are we gonna do?"

"What do you mean?" Ada asked.

"We can't let Aven marry him."

Ada's brows flew up. "Aven is much too clever to ever marry the likes of him. Don't worry about that. I'd rather live in a tent and eat one meal a day than be beholding to Archie Mitchell." She shuddered.

"Good, I can't imagine what it would be like if we had to live with him." Amelia couldn't keep the fear from her eyes. "He smells bad."

"I wish Mr. Hart would marry Aven." Ada grinned.

"The sheriff?"

"Yes, he's a kind man. Don't you think they'd make a good match?"

"I don't know." Amelia frowned. "Better than him though." She gestured to the door.

"Alright, back to your school work."

"Awwww. I hate learning history."

"I'll tell ya what. You finish that chapter, and I'll take you skating later on."

Amelia's face lit up. "You bet. I haven't been skating in forever. Is the pond ready?"

"Well, I saw Amy Martin and her friends skating out there yesterday and we'll avoid the thin ice."

Amelia ran to the table and picked up her book, excitedly.

Ada shook her head. Turning back to her mending she chuckled internally. *If I knew it was that easy to get her to study history, I'd do it every day.*

* * * *

"Hi, Aven." Amelia bounced into the livery.

Aven stood back from the large roan she was grooming and placed the comb on the ledge. She swiped her sleeve across her brow and frowned. "What are you two doing here?" She walked out of the pen and closed the gate on the horse. "Shouldn't you be studying young lady?"

"I said I'd take her skating if she finished her studies." Ada gripped Amelia's shoulder, in defense of her sister.

Aven managed a sideways smile and nodded at her sisters. "Just be careful, the ice is thin in places."

"Aven, stop being such a worry wart. We know how to spot thin ice." Amelia shrugged her shoulders.

"Okay, Poppet." Aven stretched her sore back. "Have a good time."

"Why don't you come with us?"

"Amelia, I'd love to. I haven't skated in years, but I have to work, darling."

"You always have to work." Amelia pouted. "We hardly see you."

Aven closed her eyes and sighed. "Darling, I have to work, so you can have the things you need. You can study and go skating, see all your friends."

"I'd rather have you." The smaller girl murmured.

"Please don't make it harder for me, Amelia. I'm doing what I must, just like Papa did."

Amelia nodded, "Alright."

"So did you just come here to tell me you're going skating?"

Ada frowned. "No, we wanted to tell you that Archie Mitchell came by the house looking for you. We didn't tell him where you were, but he threatened Amelia."

Ada's face curled up into a scowl. "He did what?"

Amelia's lip trembled and tears flooded her eyes. "He picked me up and held me close to him and said if we didn't tell where you were he'd do awful mean things to me."

"When I wouldn't tell him he threw her onto the couch and walked away. He was right surly, said he was gonna make you marry him one way or another."

"Please don't marry him, Aven." Amelia begged.

Aven grimaced. "Don't worry, I'm not planning to."

"Good, we'd much prefer you to marry the sheriff." Amelia blurted out. Ada bit her lip and Aven gasped.

"What do you mean by that?" She tried to keep the blush from her cheeks, unsuccessfully. "I'm not gonna marry the sheriff." But the delighted little flutter to her heart sent shivers through her body and the thought became somewhat appealing.

"We think you should, he's very handsome." Amelia persisted.

"Amelia, that is not a good reason to marry someone, now we'll have no more talk of marriage. I must get back to work. You two go and enjoy your skating."

"We will." Amelia grinned and the two younger girls hurried out into the snow.

Aven shook her head and returned to the roan's stall to finish the job.

"I wish I'd brought the gig," Aven muttered under her breath as she staggered home with the large basket of sheets and blankets from the boarding house. "Still, I'm grateful for the work." Mrs. Grant had offered her 2 cents per sheet and 5 cents per blanket to wash, and press each one. A rather time-consuming job, but she wouldn't complain. "All work is good work, if it means I can provide for my sisters." Most of the basket of goods that had been left for them was used up. And it was looking like a long hard winter was before them. The snows had come early looked set to stick around.

"Hello, Miss Miller." A mocking voice interrupted Aven's introspection. She didn't need to turn around to recognize that smarmy voice. She picked up her pace and continued toward her home.

Archie marched toward and gripped her by the shoulder, whipping her around. "I said hello."

Aven put down the basket because if she didn't she'd drop it for sure. *You catch more flies with honey.* She smiled at him. "Good day, Mr. Mitchell."

He sneered at her. "Don't you think it's time you call me Archie?"

"Why?" Aven tried to keep the frown from her face.

"Once we are married you won't need to be so formal."

Aven's brows flew up. "I wasn't aware we were getting married."

Archie gripped her chin roughly. "Not yet, but it's only a matter of time, I'm just being prepared."

"I'm not going to change my mind, Mr. Mitchell. I've told you I'm not interested."

"I plan to get you to change your mind." He sneered.

Aven tipped her head to the side and put her hands on her hips. "And just how are you going to do that?"

Archie gave her a sinister smile and lunged forward pulling Aven close to his body. He gripped the back of her head and forcefully kissed her. Aven's eyes grew wide, and she pushed at him trying to break free but he continued the kiss, holding her tightly.

Waves of terror and revulsion swarmed through her and she panicked and did the only thing she could think to do, she bit his lip.

He yanked himself away from her and slapped her across the face. "What'd you do that for?"

Aven put a hand to her throbbing cheek and determinedly blinked away the threatening tears. "To.... To stop you," she stammered and bent to collect her basket.

Archie grabbed her arm tightly. "I'm not finished with you yet, you go when I give you permission."

Aven's brows flew up. "This is not changing my mind." She fired at him determinedly. "You're only making my resolve stronger. I wouldn't marry you if you were the last man on this earth." She yanked her arm free, snatched up the basket and hurried away as quickly as she could manage with the cumbersome load.

"I will have my way, Aven Miller," he yelled at her. The game was becoming more fun now, the more she turned him down the more determined he became that she would eventually succumb.

Aven shuddered and turned the corner toward her homestead, not stopping until she got to her home. She dropped the basket on the porch and flung open the door. Stepping inside she kicked off her boots, flung her coat on the hook and hurried to her room. She closed the door behind her, threw herself down on her bed and began to weep. "Lord, please help me." She didn't know what else to ask. But the Lord knew all and He would fill in the blanks and answer her prayer in His way, in His timing. All she had to do was trust Him. She wiped her eyes and quoted, "Trust in the Lord with all thine heart; and lean not unto thine own understanding. In all thy ways acknowledge Him, and He shall direct thy paths." She smiled and looked across to her bible sitting open on her desk. "Yes Lord, I trust You'll help me to find my path. I trust you."

She hurried to change out of her dirty work clothes and into a housedress with a starched apron over the top. Forcing all thoughts of that revolting man out of her mind she went to work on the boarding house laundry. A smile crossed her face as she recalled Amelia's words. "You should marry the sheriff" That same feeling washed over that had struck her at the livery. She put both hands to her hot cheeks and grinned. "Watch you don't get ahead of yourself." She scolded, and hurried to the kitchen. But despite her best efforts her mind ran away with her while she worked.

Fifteen

"Heeeellllllppppp."

Aven's head snapped up. "Ada?" She ran to the door as the terrified voice grew closer. Hauling it open she ran out to find Ada stumbling and tripping, her younger sister in her arms, sodden.

Aven sprinted across the yard, through the snow and lifted Amelia from her exhausted sister's arms. The little girl's body was limp and cold and she still wore her skates.

Tears streamed down Ada's cheeks and she struggled to catch her breath. "She... She fell in... I... I... I tried... to warn her, but she..."

"It's alright, Ada, it's not your fault. It was just an accident. Get the door and get her skates off we have to get her warm."

Ada ran up the stairs and pushed the door open. Aven held the girl while Ada quickly untied her skates and thrust them over the hook by the door.

"Turn down her bed, I'll get some dry clothes on her."

Ada ran to comply while Aven lay her sister on the chaise and removed her wet things. Ada hurried back to help and they soon had Amelia in dry clothes tucked into a warm bed. The little girl had done little more than whimper.

"Let's get her warmed up. I hope we can avoid fever." Aven pulled the blankets up around Amelia's neck and leaned down to kiss her damp forehead.

Amelia whimpered and turned her head to the other side.

Ada slumped into the chair next to her bed. "What are we going to do?"

"What do you mean?" Aven asked.

"I mean, if she's really sick, what will we do?"

"Cross that bridge when it comes to it. She might be completely fine, let's just work on getting her warm. If she goes down hill I'll fetch Mrs. Grant."

"Mrs. Grant is a midwife."

"Yes but you know she's tended to our cuts and scrapes over the years."

"We could get the doctor from Cloudy Ridge."

Aven raised her eyebrows at her sister.

"What?" Ada frowned.

"How could we afford to pay a doctor?"

"Sometimes people pay in chickens and produce."

"Do you see spare chickens and produce around here?"

Ada sighed. "No."

"Don't make trouble, Ada. She's just as likely to be fine in a few days. She wasn't in the water long, and we got her out of her wet things and in bed."

"You're right. Now, I'll go finish supper."

Aven nodded. "That's a good idea, we both need to stay strong for Amelia."

Ada bent down and kissed Aven's forehead. "Thank you, sister."

"Ada, Ada, wake up." Aven shook her younger sister.

Ada sat up and rubbed her eyes. "What? What is it? Has Amelia woken up?"

Aven shook her head. "Not yet, she's still warm and she's groaned a few times but there's been little change."

Ada nodded.

"I need you to sit with her. I have to go to work at the saloon."

"You're still going?"

"Of course."

"I thought you'd stay home and take care of Amelia."

"Ada, we still have to eat, I have to work."

Ada frowned. "But you've had no sleep."

"I got a little." Aven shrugged. "I'll be alright."

"Alright. But please don't overdo it. I need you."

Aven kissed her sister's forehead. "I need you too, darling."

"I'll be out in a moment."

"If there are any changes, just come for me, or go straight to Mrs. Grant."

"I understand."

"Alright, I'll see you after work."

Ada smiled and swung her legs over the side of the bed.

* * * *

"Good morning, Mrs. Grant." Aven placed the heavy basket down and exhaled loudly.

"You look positively beat, girl. Sit down for a moment." The older lady pulled a chair out.

"No, I can't, I don't have time. I have to get my work done quickly so I can get back to Amelia."

Mrs. Grant smiled. "I understand. Just mind you don't overdo it, you'll be no good to anyone if you collapse."

Aven shrugged her shoulders and let out a deep sigh. "What choice do I have?"

Mrs. Grant gave her a sympathetic smile and patted her hand. She had no answers for the young woman. "You've done a good job with this. Thank you. Wait here and I'll get ya money."

"Thank you."

Mrs. Grant walked into the room and slipped Aven a few coins.

"I appreciate it, thank you for the work. Now I must get going. Franky needs me at the livery.

* * * *

"You've picked up the job well, Hart." Sheriff O'Reilly thrust a coffee cup into his hands.

"Thanks, I feel somewhat out of my depth though, I'm not sure I'm really cut out for this work."

"You'll be fine, just gotta be familiar with the law, be impartial and try your best to solve disputes without a gun where you can."

"You're a fine sheriff and a good man, Sir."

O'Reilly shrugged. "Just try to do my best with the Good Lord's help. Too many dishonest lawmen out here. No excuse for it, none at all."

"I admire your character and integrity."

Before either could respond, Bertie Williams ran in. "Telegram for you, Sheriff, marked urgent."

The sheriff nodded to the boy. "Thanks, Son."

The boy returned his nod, smiled at Austen then scampered out.

The sheriff perused the telegram and looked up at Austen. "Come on, we got some investigating to do."

"What is it?" Austen followed him to the door.

"Stage robbery, there's been a string of 'em in these parts, Burton from Arthurs Gully is asking for our help."

Austen nodded and the two men climbed on horses and headed out of town.

As always in the long silent miles in the saddle his mind drifted to home. *Home.* Austen smiled at the thought. *Is Theif River Canyon really home? They say home is where the heart is? Where is my heart?* His smile grew wider. *Perhaps its not where is my heart, so much as 'who' is my heart.* A beautiful woman with dark hair and deep brown eyes drifted into his mind. He nodded without realizing he'd done so. "I certainly think she could be my heart," he murmured.

"What'd you say?" The sheriff turned to him.

Austen's cheeks reddened and he stammered for an answer. "Ohh. I was just thinking... It was... I dunno... it was nothing really."

The sheriff lifted an eyebrow and laughed out loud. "I see. Thinking about ya girlie?"

Austen merely shrugged. "Perhaps."

The sheriff scoffed. "Well, keep your head out of the clouds, I need you alert to watch my back."

"I will be sheriff."

"Good, now come on, it's just over this hill."

*　　*　　*　　*

Aven had barely stepped through the door when Ada came running out of their sister's bedroom "Aven. You have to come quickly."

"What is it?"

"Amelia's real sick."

Aven gasped and followed her into Amelia's bedroom. The little girl was pale, she tossed and turned and groaned but remained unconscious. A cool cloth lay across her forehead.

"How long has she been feverish like this?" Aven's worry was etched into the furrow of her brows. She dabbed at her sister's cheeks with the cool cloth. "She's burning up."

"A few hours. I didn't know what to do. I couldn't leave her." Ada looked defeated.

Aven took a deep breath and petitioned the Lord for wisdom. "We have to get her to town, we are too isolated here."

"But where, there aint no clinic in town?"

"We'll take her to the boarding house. Mrs. Grant can help us."

Ada nodded.

"I'll hitch the gig, you get her in warm clothes, wrap a blanket around her. Bring some pillows, we'll have to put her on the back of the wagon."

"Is it safe to move her?" Ada was almost in tears.

"I don't know what other choice we have. We need help and we'll have more chance of that in town. Now do as I said. I'll fetch the wagon." Aven ran back out the door.

*   *   *   *

Mrs. Grant applied another cool cloth to the little girl's forehead. "She's burning up."

"Have you seen this before?" Aven couldn't keep the worry from her voice.

"I don't know, fever can happen for a lot of reasons. She's likely developing pneumonia."

"Can you fix her?" Ada asked.

"I'll do what I can, but I ain't a doctor."

"We could never afford to pay a doctor." Aven grimaced.

"There ain't no doctors in these parts nohow." Mrs. Grant bit her lip before blurting out Austen's secret.

Mrs. Grant shrugged. "I'll try." She didn't know what else to say, she was hopelessly out of her depth. *If only Mr. Hart were here. He'd know what this is and how to fight it.* "Aven, go into the living room and fetch the book of ailments from the shelf. It's a large brown leather book. I'll see if it has any idea what we should do."

Aven nodded and hurried from the room. Mrs. Grant turned to Ada. "Go and find Mrs. Watson for me please."

Ada leapt from her chair and bolted out of the room so fast she nearly crashed right into Aven approaching. "Woooow. Slow down."

"Sorry, Mrs. Grant sent me to find Mrs. Watson."

"I know, but you need to slow down, we don't need you getting injured too."

"Okay." Ada managed a shaky smile.

"Mrs. Watson is doing the wash. I saw her walking toward the back porch to hang the sheets there since it's covered in."

Ada nodded and hurried away.

"Slow down." Aven called to her.

Ada slowed to a fast walk.

Aven shook her head and entered the bedroom. Mrs. Grant had the little girls dress opened and was sponging her chest and neck. She looked up at Aven, put down the sponge and lifted the blankets back up to her neck.

Aven placed the book on a high table near the bed and positioned the lamp so they could clearly see in the dingy room.

Mrs. Grant ran her finger down a page, stopping at an entry she tapped the page twice. "It could be influenza?"

"She had it when she was small."

"You can get it more'n once, seems like theres different kinds."

"Is that what you think it is?"

Mrs. Grant flicked to another page and read an entry. "Or maybe pneumonia."

"How can we know which it is?"

"It may be neither. I've never seen a rash like that."

"A rash? Is it measles?"

Mrs. Grant turned to the entry about measles. "No, I don't think it's measles, see here a diagram of what measles looks like. This isn't like that."

"What can we do?" Aven's voice chocked a little.

"She needs a doctor."

"Where will we find a doctor, or the money to pay one?"

Mrs. Grant grimaced and gave the woman a defeated shrug. "Let's work on the assumption that it is the grippe, I've seen rashes like this with the grippe. First thing we need to do is get that fever down. Fetch me some ice." Aven nodded and dashed out.

Ada returned with Mrs. Watson in tow. Mrs. Grant smiled at the woman and her baby. "I need you to see the fires get stoked up and the two big basins of water on to boil. Then I'm going to need you to start on supper for the borders. Mrs. Blaine and Mrs. Tapper will help you, if you ask them. You know they filled in when I had the grippe a few years back."

The young woman nodded and walked away to oblige.

*　*　*　*

"You get some sleep Miss Miller. I'll watch after the little girl."

"I have to work."

"You're exhausted, been up most of the night with her."

"I've got to. I have to pay for our room and board here, and you can't take care of her forever. I might have to hire some help."

"Room and board don't matter..."

Aven cut her off. "Mrs. Grant, you can't afford three extra mouths to feed, we have to pay our way."

Mrs. Grant wanted to protest but she knew Aven was right, she was barely making ends meet herself. She gave Aven a resigned smile. "I'm sorry! I wish things were different."

Aven walked over and gripped the woman's shoulder. "You've done more than anyone could expect. Amelia is my responsibility. And Ada can't be expected to work all the time and take care of Amelia. So, it falls on me."

Mrs. Grant nodded.

*　*　*　*

"She's stable." Mrs. Grant sighed with relief and leaned back into her chair. "We've got her fever down for now, but we'll have to keep monitoring her."

"Is she out of danger?" Ada looked up from her mending.

"I won't lie to you, I don't rightly know. For now she's stopped the fitting. But we still don't know what this is."

Ada brushed away a tear that escaped down her face. "Please don't let her die? I couldn't bare to lose a sister as well as my parents."

Mrs. Grant stood and put her arm around Ada. "Keep up the prayers, God's watching over you all."

"I wish Aven would let me work."

"Then who would look after Amelia?"

Ada put down her needlework and sniffed back her tears. "I just feel so useless."

"I know, darling, but you are doing the right thing. You've been here for your sister all the time, and she needs ya."

*   *   *   *

"Much obliged to ya, Sheriff." Mr. George Connelly put his hand out to shake.

Sheriff O'Reilly shook the offered hand and then Austen followed suit. "Just doing my job, sir, the men are behind bars and we're returning people's property where we can."

Mr. Connelly turned the jewels and rings over in his hands. "It makes my Jenny seem so much closer to me." He swiped at his eyes with the back of his rough hand.

The Sheriff gripped his shoulder. "I'm sorry we couldn't bring her back to you, George. She was a good woman."

"Thank you, Sheriff. Just knowing those men are in custody means a lot to me."

"It's Hart you really ought to thank. He's the one that found the clues that led us to catching them."

"Oh, I was just doing my job..." Austen's words seemed feeble so he stopped and shrugged.

"I thank you. I'd like to do something to show my gratitude for returning my Jenny's things."

"That's not necessary, I was doing my job."

"Please, young man, there must be something I can do for you?"

Austen turned his head to look toward the barn. His eyes lit up and he smiled. "Would you consider selling the sleigh?"

Sixteen

Mrs. Watson knocked at the door, startling Aven awake. "Ohh, what, sorry. I fell asleep. What is it Mrs. Watson."

"I'm sorry that I woke ya. Mrs. Grant wants ya to come out to the dining room. She has a guest she wants you to meet."

"I'm not dressed for company, and I don't want to leave Amelia, she's had a rough night."

"It'll just take a minute. I'll sit with her if you like."

"Would you?"

Mrs. Watson smiled. "I'd be happy to."

Aven stood, kissed her sister's brow and squeezed her arm. Amelia groaned and turned her head. "I'll be right back, darling." Aven left the room and headed out to the dining room.

"Aven." Mrs. Grant gestured to her. "I'd like you to me Miss Lily Allen Cunningham.

Aven gave her a slight frown. "Hello."

"Hello, Miss Miller, Mrs. Grant's been telling me about your younger sister."

"She has?" Aven slumped down in the chair and gave them both quizzical looks.

Mrs. Grant touched Aven's arm. "I'm sorry, I should explain. Miss Cunningham has just arrived in town, she's staying at the boarding house for a time."

Aven gave her a polite smile. "Welcome to Theif River Canyon."

"Thank you." The young woman said.

"Well, it's lovely to meet you but I have to get back to my sister." Aven began to stand.

"Wait, Miss Miller. Mrs. Grant has only given you half the story. You see I'm only passing through. I'm on my way to California, my brother is a doctor out there and I'm on my way to join him in his clinic."

Aven frowned.

"I'm a nurse, Miss Miller."

Aven's eyes lit up. "A nurse?"

"Yes, Ma'am. Worked three years in a hospital back east."

Tears flooded the corners of Aven's eyes. "You are an answer to prayer Miss Cunningham. Would you look in on my sister."

"I'd be happy to, I'll be here for a few days."

"I'm much obliged to you. I don't have much money but I'll get it."

Mrs. Watson came hurrying out. "The little girl, she's fitting again."

"Oh." Aven leapt out of her chair.

"Take me to her." Miss Cunningham stood.

"Don't you want to rest for a time." Mrs. Grant asked.

"No, a patient needs me." Lily hastened to follow Aven. Immediately bending over the writhing girl, she examined her.

Amelia groaned and sweat poured from her face.

Lily unbuttoned the girl's blouse and exposed her chest. "Oh... how long has she had this rash?"

"Came on about two weeks ago." Aven gripped her sister's sweaty hand.

"And how long was that after she fell in the river?"

"About three days."

"Does she have any cuts anywhere on her body?"

"Not that I know of."

"I'll examine her. Would you all wait outside, so I can work."

"Sure. Come on Ada." Aven put her hand out to her sister. "Let's leave Miss Cunningham for a moment."

"But..."

"Ada, please, she knows what she's doing. She's gonna help Amelia."

Mrs. Grant refilled the coffee cups and sat down with Aven and Ada while they waited. It was some time before Lily walked out. She nodded to them and took a seat. Mrs. Grant gestured to the coffeepot and the nurse nodded. She stood and poured her a cup and slid it over. "I'll leave you be."

Aven gripped the woman's arm. "Won't you please stay?"

Mrs. Grant nodded and regained her seat.

All eyes swung to the nurse. "So, how is she nurse?"

Lily took a sip of her coffee and placed it down, cupping it in both hands. "I'm afraid she's a lot sicker than you know."

Ada whimpered and Aven gripped her hand. They looked up at the nurse. "Please, continue."

"I am not a doctor, but I'm almost certain your sister has blood poisoning."

"Blood poisoning? But how?"

"I found a small cut on her arm and it's badly infected, I imagine she cut herself when she fell through the ice. The wound must have got some germ in it and it's got into her blood."

"Germ?" Ada furrowed her brow.

"It's a fairly recent discovery but we now know there are these little... well, creatures I suppose, and they carry disease, they live in dirty water and dead creatures, all kinds of places even our own bodies. We come into contact with these germs all the time and usually our bodies can fight them off, but sometimes for a number of reasons the body is weak and the germ gets hold instead and causes poisoning."

"What does that mean for Amelia."

"It means, if she doesn't get help very soon, she's going to die." The woman was matter-of-fact, she wouldn't lie to a patient.

"Ohhh." Ada burst into tears.

Aven closed her eyes and drew strength from the Lord. "What do you mean? Can't you help her?"

"I'm afraid she needs hospital care. And as soon as possible."

"How soon?" Aven asked.

"Within a week at the longest, she is stable at the moment but she will continue with fits of delirium and fever for a time as the germ takes over until it finally kills her."

"But it can be treated."

"In some cases, they can do what's called a 'transfusion' where they take some of the blood from her body and replace it with blood from a healthy person."

"She can have my blood." Aven offered.

Lily smiled. "Even so, I can't do the procedure, she needs to be in a hospital, where they have the equipment."

"How much would that cost?"

"I can't say, Miss, it varies."

"Can you give me an estimate?"

"Well, in our hospital in Chicago it was Two dollars and fifty cents a week for the stay and then the procedures and nursing care on top of that, say, ten dollars a week."

Aven's lips trembled and her face fell. "Where am I going to get that kind of money?"

Lily squeezed her arm. "I'm sorry."

"Don't be." Aven swiped at her tears. "I'm grateful to you for letting us know."

"I'll care for her until I leave in three days time, but I'll just be dealing with symptoms, you need to make arrangements for her to get to hospital as soon as you can."

Aven nodded. Her whole body felt numb. *Lord, where am I going to get the money.* But God was silent and far away. "Thank you, Miss Cunningham."

"You're welcome. I'll go and sit with her for a time."

"I gotta go find some work, see if I can't raise some money for Amelia."

"I'll work too."

"No, Ada, I need you to stay with Amelia. I will work something out, I promise."

Ada gave her a resigned nod. "But I can work."

"Tell ya what. I'll pay ya to work around here, where I can. It'll be my contribution to her treatment. I'm sorry I can't give ya a lot."

"Everything helps, Mrs. Grant. I'm much obliged." Aven stood. "I'll go and check on Amelia, then I have to go and find a job. One way or another I will find the money."

Seventeen

"Whaddya want?" Archie scowled and stood to open the door. He sneered at the man. "Reverend? What brings you to my place? Come to save my soul?"

"As much as I'd love to do that, Mr. Mitchell, I've come on another matter today."

"Oh?" Archie folded his arms over his chest.

"It seems there is a rather urgent need and we are raising money."

"No." Archie sneered. "I'm not interested." He tried to shut his door.

The reverend put his foot out to stop the door. "Wait, it involves the Millers."

Archie yanked open the door. "What about the Millers..."

*   *   *   *

"You're working awful hard, Miss Miller."

Aven ignored Archie and carried right on with scrubbing the wooden floor of the saloon.

"I said, You're working awful hard."

Aven sat back on her knees. "I have to, Mr. Mitchell."

"Are you sure about that?"

"Of course, I'm sure, now if you don't mind, I have a lot to do tonight."

"The reverend told me about your sister and how you need the money."

Aven ignored him and resumed her scrubbing. "What's it to you."

"You know you don't have to work at all. I'll give you all the money you need for your sister's hospital care."

Aven gasped and sat back on her feet again. A sense of dread washed over her. "And what would you want in return?"

"You know what I want Aven, marry me and I can have your sister in the hospital before the week is spent."

A momentary 'what if' floated through her mind but then the reality shook her. "No thank you, Mr. Mitchell. I will earn the money."

"How's that going?" He scoffed.

"I've earned two dollars and thirty eight cents after this and the reverend collected another three so we are well on our way to her transport and the first weeks hospital stay." She tried to sound excited but in her heart she knew that she could never earn enough if there were five of her working round the clock.

"Seems pointless when I could give you a hundred dollars today."

"I'd appreciate that, Mr. Mitchell."

"But only if you marry me, I ain't a charity."

"I said no thank you. Now if you don't mind, I must get back to it."

"You'll come to me sooner or later. You know that you need me."

Aven concentrated on her scrubbing and ignored him. Archie let out a loud groan and hurried away.

Aven heard the door close and sat back on her feet and shuddered. "Lord, I pray it doesn't come to that. I have to work harder and earn the money." She doubled the speed of her scrubbing.

Stumbling in at a little after midnight Aven slumped into the arm chair next to Amelia's bed. Lily was monitoring her while she slept.

"Miss Miller, you are exhausted."

Aven ignored the nurse and focused on her sister. "How is Amelia?"

"No change, she's fitted some, she's going downhill rather quickly."

"What do you mean?"

"I mean she's getting worse, Aven, I won't lie to you, unless you can get her to hospital in a few days it doesn't look good."

Aven bit her lip. "But I can't get that kind of money so soon, you don't suppose they'll let us pay later?"

"It's not common practice, they provide a service and expect to be paid."

"I understand."

"I'll be back to check on her in a few hours. If there are any changes come and get me."

"Thank you, Miss Cunningham."

"You're welcome. I'm happy to help while I'm here. Goodnight."

"Goodnight," Aven called as the nurse left. She turned to lower the lamp and leaned her head against the high back of the chair. She closed her eyes and sighed. "Lord, we need you here, the situation is dire now and we need you to intervene. I'd do anything to save my sister." She opened her eyes and looked at Amelia's face, so pale and covered in sweat. The little girl was very weak and she whimpered and moved slightly. "Anything." Aven let out a sob. She shuddered. "What other choice do I have?"

* * * *

"Why'd you buy that sleigh anyway?" Sheriff O'Reilly chuckled.

"I have my reasons." Austen sat proudly in the high seat of the sleigh and flicked the rein over the horses back as it slid smoothy over the thick snow. A wry grin crossed the younger man's face.

The sheriff caught it and eyed him knowingly. "I see, Girl reasons?"

"Something like that." Austen chuckled.

"Care to share?"

"Nope!"

The sheriff nodded. "Well I'm gonna miss having you around when you go home tomorrow."

"Me too, I've been grateful for your help, I feel much more equipped to take over the sheriff job now."

"Well you're a fast learner and you're a natural, you really care about people. You'll do well."

"Thank you."

"I can't wait to get home, just over that hill."

"I slowed us down a bit with this sleigh."

"Not too much. Your horse almost looks proud to be hauling it."

"Princess is a good horse. You wait till this sleigh is all decorated up for Christmas, it's going to be beautiful."

The sheriff smiled. "I bet it makes that girlie fall head over heels in love with you."

"I can only pray and hope."

At long last just before midday they pulled up outside the sheriff's office in Cloudy Ridge. "You want some coffee, rest a little before we see to the horses?" The sheriff dismounted and hooked his horses rein over the hitching post.

"Sure." Austen jumped down from the sleigh and tethered his horse too.

"Say, Sheriff." Alexander Price waved and ran across to them.

The two men swivelled on their heels as the postman ran up.

The sheriff raised his brows.

"I'm glad you're back, this telegram came for you two days ago."

The sheriff reached for it but Alex shook his head. "No not you, it's for Sheriff Hart."

"Me?" Austen frowned.

The postman passed it to Austen, nodded and turned to walk away.

"Thank you."

The man lifted his hand in the air in response and stepped into the post office.

Austen slipped the paper from the envelope.

"OH!" He looked up at the sheriff. "I gotta get back to Theif River Falls, right away."

"Are you sure?"

"Yeah, I have to, she needs me."

Sheriff O'Reilly nodded. "Don't you want your things."

"Keep it, I'll get more. I can't wait, thanks for everything." Austen leapt up on the sleigh. The telegram fell to the ground as he clucked to Princess and hurried out of town as fast the horse could manage.

The sheriff waved to Austen then turned to walk inside. He stopped, picked up the telegram and read it.

MR. HART

AMELIA MILLER DANGEROUSLY ILL. PLEASE COME AT ONCE.

ELEANOR. T. GRANT

The sheriff shrugged. "I hope you get there in time lad." He grimaced. "I hope that's not your girlie." He shook his head and walked back into the office.

Eighteen

"You don't have to do this." Mrs. Grant offered.

Aven's lip trembled. "I don't have any other choice."

"There must be something else you can do? Anything else?"

"I'm open to suggestions. I've worked myself to the bone, the reverend has asked for donations and we haven't got more'n eight dollars for our trouble. That will barely cover the transport to get there."

"But marrying Archie Mitchell?"

Aven swiped at her tears. "What choice do I have. He will pay for Amelia's treatment."

"But marriage, you'll be attached to that vile man forever."

Aven took a deep breath. "I know. But its for Amelia, she's worth it. I'd rather spend my life attached to that... that man, than lose my sister."

Mrs. Grant nodded and gave her a sympathetic smile. "I'm sorry, Aven, truly. If there was anything I could do..."

"I know Mrs. Grant. It's alright, you've been more than kind."

"Your Mama was my friend. I'll always look out for you girls however I can."

"Well, I do appreciate you helping me pack my things." Aven looked around her small house. "I suppose my surroundings will be different tonight."

"He does have a nice house." Mrs. Grant grasped for the one positive she could find.

"Yes. I wish there was a way I didn't have to bring the girls with me, I don't know what he might do to them."

"They could stay at the boarding house with me?"

"I'd be obliged if Ada could stay with you at least until Amelia is out of hospital. She'll earn her keep."

"She can stay as long as you need her."

"Thank you. You've been a good friend."

"It's a shame there are no flowers at this time of year."

"I don't want flowers. I don't want to pretend this is a happy marriage."

"I hope you don't regret this."

"I will regret it every day of my life, Mrs. Grant, but my sister is worth it."

Mrs. Grant dropped the subject. They locked the door to the cabin and climbed up into the gig.

*   *   *   *

Austen flew up the stairs of the cabin and knocked on the door. There was no response. "Aven," he called as loudly as he could. Peering in the window it didn't appear anyone was home and the fire wasn't going. "Perhaps they are all in town." He jumped back up on the sleigh and headed for the livery to discard the sleigh, he could move faster on horseback. He galloped to the boarding house as fast as his tired horse could manage.

Flicking the rein over the rail he ran inside and hurried into the kitchen. "Mrs. Grant."

"Oh, Mr. Hart, thank the Lord you're here." Mrs. Grant lifted the coffeepot and he gave her a grateful look.

"How's the little girl?"

"The nurse that's here visiting said she has blood poisoning."

"Ohhh." Austen nodded. "May I see her?"

"Of course." She gestured to the room.

Austen knocked on the open door and walked in. The nurse placed the cool cloth on the girls forehead and looked up. "Can I help you, sir?... ah.. Sheriff."

He looked down at his badge and back up at her. "I'm Hart, Mr.... ahhh, Dr. Hart."

"Oh, you must be the man Mrs. Grant told me of, she said she sent you a telegram?"

"Yes." He frowned. *So much for that secret.*

"Don't worry, I'm sworn to secrecy."

He nodded. "Tell me her symptoms."

Mrs. Grant entered the room and passed him a cup of coffee. He nodded his thanks. "I believe your diagnosis is correct, Nurse, she has blood poisoning."

"Can you treat her?"

"Yes, I believe I can if I can get the equipment I need."

"That's such a relief. Aven has been beside herself trying to raise money."

"Money?" Austen frowned.

"For the hospital." Mrs. Grant gestured. "She's most anxious."

"Oh no. I think we can keep the girl out of hospital, if we get her treatment right away. There is no time to lose. I'll get my kit." He couldn't understand why he'd kept it, but it was tucked at the bottom of his bag and had most of what he needed, the rest he could send for.

"We wired the hospital, and sent for a doctor but it was much too expensive. Aven could never afford to get a doctor here or take Amelia to the doctor."

Austen raised his brows.

"Mr. Hart, you know the Millers don't have that kind of money, we've fundraised some but she hasn't come close to meeting the cost. And they refused to send a doctor without the promise of pay."

He frowned. "We'll find a way. Where is Aven anyway?"

"Last I knew she was waiting on the reverend? He's due back from the Hickman Homestead soon, then they'll have the weddin'" Mrs. Grant bit her lip.

Austen's brows flew up. "Wedding?"

"Yes. Miss Aven is marrying that Mitchell chap. He offered to pay her sisters medical costs if she'd marry him."

A knife stabbed Austen's heart. "And she agreed?" He felt like he was going to choke.

Mrs. Grant shrugged. "She didn't think she had a choice, her sister will die without a doctor and she was stuck."

"Well I gotta stop it. Where is she?"

"I believe they're both waiting at the church, the reverend is going to meet them there any moment."

"Nurse, will you watch the patient? I'll be right back?"

The nurse nodded. "Of course, doctor."

"What are you gonna do?" Mrs. Grant asked.

"I don't know yet, but one thing's for certain I will NOT let her marry him."

Mrs. Grant grinned. "Good luck, boy."

He nodded and turned on his heels, sprinted out the door and leapt onto the sleigh. "Sorry Girl, I know you're tired but this is an emergency."

He pulled up outside the church, leapt down and flew up the stairs.

"...do you Archibald Mitchell take this woman..." The reverend's head flicked up as the door flung open and Austen hurried in.

"Wait, stop. Don't do it!"

Aven spun her head around. "Austen?"

"Don't do this, Aven, don't marry him."

"I have to." She sobbed, "it's the only way."

"No, you don't have to. I promise, it's not the only way."

Archie walked up and grabbed her arm. "If you don't mind the reverend is waiting..."

Austen stepped in front of her. "No, she's not marrying you."

Archie raised his brows. "Excuse me? How does this have anything to do with you?"

"She's my fiancée, she's promised to me."

Austen ignored him and turned to face her, blocking her from him. "Do you want to marry him?" He kept his voice low.

She looked at him and shook her head. "I have no other choice." Tears flooded her eyes.

"If there was another way, would you take it?" The sincerity in her eyes convinced her she could trust him.

"But there is no other way." The tears overflowed. "If I can't get medical care for Amelia, she's going to die..."

"You're too late, she's agreed to marry me." Archie growled.

Austen spun around. "If you don't mind, the lady and I are having a conversation." Without waiting for a response he turned back to her. "There is another way. I promise you." He looked into her eyes and reached up to brush a tear off her cheek. "Trust me, everything will be fine, I won't let your sister die. I promise, but you must not marry this man."

Aven's lip trembled and she looked up at Archie, then back at Austen she burst into tears and threw herself into his arms. "I trust you," she managed.

"Come on, let's go to Amelia."

"But... how will you manage that without me?" Archie stormed. "You need me."

"I will take care of it, Mr. Mitchell. Aven is no longer in need of you. I will take care of her and her sisters."

Aven sighed as a wave of relief ran through her body.

"Fine, go, but you'll be sorry. When you can't pay your sister's medical bills or find a doctor for her, don't come crying to me, you ungrateful..." But Aven and Austen were already out the door.

He paused as the door closed on Archie. "Aven, I need you to trust me. I promise all will be well. I'll explain as we go but I can assure you I will take care of you." He smiled and lifted a hand to cup her cheek, willing her to get his meaning.

"And my sisters?"

"Of course."

"Oh, Austen." She placed her head against his chest and he wrapped his arms around her and kissed her hair.

"Come on. We have to get to your sister." He lifted her up onto Princess's back and climbed up in front of her.

She clung to his waist. "But she needs a doctor, where will we find a doctor and how will we pay for it." Austen could hear the tremble in her voice.

"Trust me, Aven. Please?"

She lay her head against his back, "I trust you."

Austen clucked to Princess and they rode away. He was certain he heard Aven whisper, 'cherished' as they left the church yard. He smiled, that was a wonderful word, it described exactly how he felt about her perfectly.

Aven pulled Princess to a stop outside the boarding house and climbed down. He reached up both hands to Aven. She put her hands on his shoulders and slipped down into his arms. They locked eyes and the intensity of the moment made Austen's heart speed up. There was so much he wanted to say to her, but he swallowed back those feelings. The priority was Amelia, he was just grateful that she hadn't had to marry that man.

He paused for a moment and smiled. "Come on, let's get to your sister." He offered her his hand and she smiled and took it and allowed him to lead her inside. They hurried to Amelia's bedside.

"How is she nurse?"

"No change, Doctor." Lily said without thinking, then bit her lip.

Austen closed his eyes, and Aven's eyes grew wide and her mouth dropped open. "You're a..."

Austen stopped her with a nod. "Yes, I'm a doctor. Trained back east. I'll explain later, I promise, but for now, will you allow to help your sister?"

Tears flooded Aven's eyes and her lips trembled. She threw herself in his arms. "Thank you, oh, thank you."

Austen closed his eyes, and cradled her head. "It's my pleasure."

She released him. "You're an answer to prayer."

Austen smiled and gave her a nod.

"What do you need me to do, Doctor?" Lily asked.

"I'll make you a list, could you go to the store. What Jensen doesn't have we'll have to order in, we should be able to get in on tomorrow's stage."

"I'll fetch a note pad." The nurse left the room.

Aven put a hand on Austen's arm and looked him in the eye. "Are you really here or am I dreaming?"

"I'm really here, Aven."

"Why didn't you tell anyone you're a doctor?"

He closed his eyes and sighed. "It's a long story, I promise to tell you everything, but for now let's concentrate on getting Amelia well."

Aven smiled and tears flooded her eyes again. She stood up on her toes put her hand on his shoulder and kissed his cheek. "Thank you."

He grinned. "As much as I liked that, you don't have to keep thanking me. It's the least I can do for you."

Aven smiled. "Well I want you to know, I'm grateful to you."

"It's my pleasure." He smiled to the nurse as she entered the room and passed him a note pad. He wrote down a few entries, tapped his chin with the pencil as he thought. It'd been a long time since he'd done the procedure and he had no access to a well-stocked hospital. He'd have to improvise. Adding two more entries to the list he passed it back to her.

Lily perused it. "I'll be right back."

"We'll get the little girl ready."

The nurse nodded and hurried out of the room.

"What do you need me to do?" Aven asked.

"We need to find a healthy person to donate some blood. I'd do it, happily but it really should be a woman. The procedure has more chance when it's woman to woman or man to man."

"I'll do it."

"Oh, I wasn't thinking you'd do it, I just thought you might suggest someone."

165

"I'll do it, please, she's my sister."

"Are you sure, it'll be very unpleasant."

"Austen, I'd do anything for my sister, I was willing to marry that man." She shuddered at the thought. "For her."

"You're a brave woman."

"I'm not so brave. I'm just doing what I need to for my family."

"Yes, I've seen how hard you've worked for them."

"And I'll continue to do so as long as I draw breath."

"I don't doubt that for a moment."

"What do you need me to do?"

"Could you change your clothes?"

Aven frowned. "how come?"

"I'll need to get to your arm for the transfusion."

Aven nodded. "I understand. I'll find a blouse with looser sleeves."

"Great. I'll get your sister ready. Say where is your other sister?"

"I convinced Ada to take a day off. She's off at Lacey Anders skating. I didn't want her to know I was going to marry Mr. Mitchell. I was just going to tell her when it was done."

"I'm so glad you didn't have to do that."

"Thanks to you." She smiled. "I'll go change my dress."

Austen nodded and watched her walk away. He left to scrub his hands and he took a few moments to pray. "Lord, I'm gonna need your help, I pray this works."

The nurse arrived back. "He had everything except the tubes, but he wondered if this rubber tubing from these bottles will work?"

Austen took them from her hand and examined them. "If we could join them, they'd work."

"Could you, melt them together?"

"We'll try it, thanks nurse."

"Whatever you need, Doctor."

"I'll need you to monitor both Aven and Amelia throughout the procedure."

"I understand."

Aven entered the room. "I'm ready doctor." She had her sleeves rolled up as high as they would go.

"Very good." Austen smiled. "Lie down up there next to your sister."

Aven did as he asked and Austen gently gripped her arm. "Are you comfortable?"

"Yes."

Nineteen

"Thanks for accompanying me, this morning. It's good to get you out of that room and out into the crisp winter air." Austen lead Aven toward the frozen lake.

"Now that Amelia is on the mend I feel like I can finally breath again. Thanks to you."

"You don't need to thank me. It was my pleasure."

"I guess she'll be coming home soon and I can get back to work."

"Work?"

"I have three jobs you know, we still have to eat?"

"I wish you didn't have to work so hard."

"I have to Austen, I have my sisters to consider. We can't mooch off Mrs. Grant and your generosity forever, I need to repay you."

"Repay me?"

"For all the work you've done for Amelia, all your time and your medicines." They stopped at the log by the frozen lake, it shone in the moonlight leaving a bright glow on the icy surface.

"Aven, you don't owe me anything."

"But you've done so much for us..."

Austen stopped her by taking both her hands in his. "I did those things for you because I wanted to."

"You've been so kind to us."

"It's my pleasure."

She leaned into him and put her arms around his chest. "Thank you for giving me back my sister."

"It's my pleasure." He repeated. Her hug had completely caught him off guard and his heart pounded so hard he couldn't find any better words.

She clung to him for some time and he relished his arms being around her. It was wonderful to hold her, she was everything he dreamed of and more.

Aven felt so comfortable in his arms, she never wanted to leave them. "It's so beautiful out here. I love this time of year." She murmured against his chest.

"Yes it is."

"I can't believe Christmas is only a few weeks away."

"Yes and your sister will be up and about by then."

"I'm glad." Aven stepped back from him. "Thanks to you." She stepped up on her toes and kissed his cheek.

Austen grinned at her. "What was that for?"

"To say thank you. You're a wonderful doctor, you really should open a clinic."

"I can't. You know why."

"But you're so gifted, can't you put that behind you?"

"I couldn't save her, Aven, I couldn't save my own fiancée."

"But you saved Amelia?"

"This time, what about the next time?"

"What next time?"

"Eventually a patient is bound to die."

"So."

"So? I can't bear to think people die at my hand."

"You're giving yourself a lot of credit."

Austen frowned at her. "What do you mean by that?"

"It's not up to you who lives and dies it's up to God."

"But I'm the one doing the doctoring."

"Austen, no matter how good of a doctor you are, if the Lord wants to call someone home there is no stopping him. You have to let go of Harriet. You know as well as I do you're not suited to being sheriff, you're much more suited to being a doctor."

Austen sighed loudly. "I'm scared."

"I know. But you needn't be, you can only do your very best and let the Lord be your guide."

He managed a sideways smile and nodded. "I'll think on it."

"Good, because this town needs you. I need you." She hung her head shyly and looked at her boots in the moonlight.

Austen grinned and lifted her chin so he could look her in the eye. "Aven?"

"Yes?"

"Would you let me take you out for supper tomorrow night?"

"Why tomorrow particularly?" She squinted at him.

"I heard it was your birthday." He grinned at her.

Aven squinted at him. "Who told you that?"

"Ada."

"That little sneak."

"Well, will you?"

"Where do you want to go."

"I have it all arranged. Don't you worry."

"Alright."

"I'll meet you out front of the boarding house at five pm."

Aven smiled. "Alright."

Austen grinned. "I'll see you then. Now let me walk you back to your room. I'll check in on Amelia but I'm fairly confident she'll be up in a few days."

Aven took his outstretched elbow and they turned back toward the boarding house. "I'm glad.

*   *   *   *

"Doctor Hart said you could get up tomorrow, darling." Aven passed her younger sister a sandwich.

"I can't wait." Amelia grinned. "I feel like I've been in bed forever. I'm so glad I'll be up and about before Christmas. I wish I was up in time for your birthday. It's not fun celebrating from a bed."

"This is just fine. The best birthday present I could ever have gotten is you being well again. I thought I was gonna lose you."

"Aven..." A voice called from the doorway.

"I'm in here."

Ada popped her head in the door. "Aven, Mrs. Grant wants to see you."

"Oh?"

"Yes, she said something about a surprise?"

Aven pursed her lips. "I wish she wouldn't."

"Well you better go tell her, then." A wide grin lit up Ada's face.

"What are you hiding, Sister?"

"Nothing. Go and see Mrs. Grant. I'll stay with Amelia."

Aven grinned. "Alright." She stood and kissed Amelia's forehead and left the room.

"Mrs. Grant?"

"Oh, Aven." Mrs. Grant smiled. "Come with me, I have something for you."

"You didn't have to do anything for me, I told you that. You've let us stay here all this time and that's more than enough."

"It's not from me."

"It's not?" Aven frowned.

"Nope."

Aven shrugged and followed Mrs. Grant into her room. Lying on her bed was a beautiful lavender colored gown and a long fur coat. "These are for you."

Aven cupped her hand over her mouth. "What? How come?"

Mrs. Grant shrugged. "I don't know. A messenger delivered these for you, came off this mornings stagecoach. I had it laid out for you."

"But, what? Who?"

"I don't know but I think you ought to wear them tonight?"

"For my birthday supper?"

"Mmmhmmm."

"Did Austen organize these?"

"I don't know anything about that but I'm not sure what he'd know about dresses."

"Well I suppose I should bathe and get ready." Aven clasped her hands together.

Emerging from her room an hour later, Aven walked into the dining room. "Will I do?"

Mrs. Grant leapt up from her chair and discarded the potatoes she was peeling. "You'll more than do, Miss Aven, you're gonna knock his stockings off. That beautiful dress, your pretty hair and your eyes glowing so, you'll make him weak at the knees."

"Oh stop it."

"It's true, Aven you look like an angel." Ada hurried over and embraced her sister.

"Thank you, Dear."

"Now, I've been told that I'm supposed to escort you to the door."

"What's going on?" Aven grimaced.

"You'll see, Sister."

Aven smiled and let Ada lead her to the door.

They stood out on the wide porch in the moonlight. "It's such a beautiful clear night. And not too cold."

"It's perfect."

"Perfect for what."

"You'll see."

"I thought Austen was going to meet me here? It's a little strange, he lives in the boarding house but I haven't seen him since breakfast."

"The town looks so pretty all decorated for Christmas."

"Yes, I sure do love this time of ye..." They both turned abruptly as the sound of bells jingled on the air. "What on earth?"

Ada smiled. She stood up on her toes and kissed her sister's cheek. "Happy Birthday, Sister." She snuck back into the boarding house and closed the door.

Ada shrugged and stood waiting, enjoying the view of the night. The bells got louder and she craned her head in the direction they came from and her mouth dropped open and her eyes grew wide. Tears streamed down her face as a sleigh came around the corner drawn by two white horses. Austen pulled up in front of the boarding house and pulled the horses to a stop.

He jumped down and walked up the stairs wearing a handsome navy suit. He put his hand out to her. "Your carriage awaits my lady."

Aven could do little more than smile and sniff away tears. She took a deep breath and found her voice. "What is this?"

"Your carriage." He gestured to the sleigh, freshly painted and decorated with boughs of holly and ribbon, bells hung from the pine boughs. Even the horses had ribbons around their necks and bells on their bridles.

"Ohhhh. Austen, this is so wonderful."

He grinned. "You said you always wanted to ride in a two horse sleigh."

"Thank you."

"You're welcome." He put his hand out to her and helped her up into the sleigh.

He climbed up next to her and clicked to the horses. Aven tucked her hand under his arm. "Where are we going?"

"You'll see."

They headed in the direction of the lake and as they turned the corner and the lake came into view, Aven gasped. "What is all this?"

In the midst of the frozen lake was a table and chairs, set with a table cloth and dishes, a small area was ringed with logs and candles in glass jars sitting all around on top. A canopy of bunting and ribbons hung above.

Austen pulled the sleigh to a stop and jumped out. He put his hand out to her and helped her down. "It's your very own ice-ball."

"Ohhhh, Austen." Aven's eyes flooded with tears. "This is wonderful, but I'm not wearing the right shoes for skating?"

"Don't worry about that." He reached into a small trunk in the back of the sleigh and pulled out a brand new pair of white lace up ice-skates. "I came prepared."

"How did you do all this?"

"I had help." He led her over to the edge of the lake. "Might I say, you look exquisite tonight."

"Thank you, someone left this dress for me."

Aven's eyes twinkled and he grinned. "I know, don't I have excellent taste."

"You got this dress for me?"

"I ordered it from Cloudy Ridge, you told me about the Ice-ball and the beautiful gown and fur coat. I wanted to recreate it all for you for your birthday. Complete with horse-drawn sleigh. Now, sit down and let me help you with these skates.

Aven sat down and unlaced her boots. Austen knelt on a small mat he placed down and slipped first one and then the other skate onto her feet and laced them up. He reached for her hand and helped her to her feet.

"Wait there." He brushed her cheek.

She nodded.

Austen walked back to the sleigh and fetched his own pair of skates. He sat down and fixed them to his boots.

"I thought you said you couldn't skate."

"I couldn't, I got lessons from a friend."

Aven grinned. "Ada? She was in on this wasn't she?"

"Yep." He put his hand out to her. "Well, miss, might I have this dance?"

"There's no music." She took his hand and they slipped out onto the lake.

"Trust me." He winked at her and glided towards the table.

"Hey you skate beautifully."

"I'm still just a beginner so be gentle with me." He smiled and flicked open a small box on the table, it was a music box and a little dancing lady began to turn around as the music played.

He reached for both her hands and they glided out to the little dancefloor under the awning. Austen pulled her into his arms and she lay her head against his chest. They glided on the ice for a time.

"Austen, why did you do all this."

"I should think it rather obvious?"

Aven stepped out of his arms to look at him.

"Why do you think?"

"I don't know."

He put his hand on her cheek. "Because I love you."

Aven smiled widely and slipped her arms around his neck. "I love you too."

Austen's face lit and he examined her face for a time, then leaned in to kiss her. He broke the kiss and lay his forehead against hers. "You really love me too?"

"Yes. I have for a time. You make me feel... oh it's silly."

"It's not silly, finish that thought."

She looked in his eyes. "Cherished."

"You are."

"I can't believe you did all this for me."

"It's the least I could do. I wanted it to be so much more, this seems a little feeble compared to what I want to do for you."

"What do you want to do?"

"I want to take care of you all your days, to not have to watch you struggle and strive all the time. To give you a happy and fulfilled life of love and joy. I want to be with you and love you as long as I draw breath and give your sister's a good home."

"What are you saying?"

"Well." He pushed back from her. "This isn't so easy wearing skates. He very carefully knelt on the ice trying desperately not to fall over. He beamed when he succeeded and reached into his pocket and pulled out a small velvet box. He flicked it open, took her hand and smiled up at her. "I want you to be my wife. Will you marry me?"

Aven grinned and tears flooded her eyes. "Yes, of course I will."

He slipped the ring on her finger and chuckled. "Could you help me up?"

"Certainly." She put both hands out to him and helped him to his feet. He stumbled for a moment and then finally regained his footing. Both burst out in laughter.

"I think we might be safer sitting down." Austen laughed.

"I think you might be right. But first." She slipped her arms around his neck. "I love you, Austen Hart."

"I love you, Aven Miller. I can't wait to marry you. How would you feel about getting married on Christmas day."

"So soon?"

"Why wait, I've loved you and watched out for you for months now. I can't bear to see you struggle, I want to give you a good life. Get a house in town and live there with your sisters. I don't want to see you have to fight for every penny."

"You've watched out for me for months? What do you mean by that?"

He grinned and raised his brows.

Aven frowned and then her face lit up. "That was you, the mystery gifts, the firewood?"

"Mmhmmm."

"And paying off our debt at the mercantile? The Doll for Amelia?"

"All of it."

"Why?"

"I told you, I couldn't bear to see you suffering. I knew you'd never accept my charity, so I did it secretly."

"I want to be angry at you but I'm so happy I could burst. Thank you."

He leaned in and kissed her deeply. "Thank you."

"But how can you afford all this?"

"Aven I'm the son of one of the wealthiest surgeons in the east."

"Are you saying you're rich?"

"I guess you could say that."

"Wow. I never would've guessed. You're so humble and kind."

"Money doesn't define me, but I'm glad I have it, so I can see to it you never go hungry again, you have all you need all your days. I mean it. I want to give you the world."

"Oh, Austen , you don't know what all this means to me. This past year and a half have been so hard, losing Mama and Papa and then struggling to make ends meet and Amelia's sickness. I shudder to think how close I came to marrying Archie Mitchell. I thought I was headed for a life of struggle and hardship and maybe that was just my lot in life..."

Austen stopped her with a kiss. "You never have to worry about that again. I promise. You and your sisters will be safe and protected with me."

Aven lay her head against his chest and he wrapped her in his arms, kissed her hair and they swayed in time with the music.

"Cherised," she murmured into his chest.

"Yes, my darling, cherished. Shall we have a drink and some cake?"

"I'd love to."

"Then I'll take you for a long ride in that sleigh, I love seeing your eyes light up the way they did."

"Thank you, Austen, for saving my life and for the sleigh. You've made all my dreams come true." She bit her lip. "There's just one thing."

"What? You can ask me anything?"

"Please don't give up on medicine? You're a fine doctor."

Austen cupped her cheek and kissed her deeply. "I'll need your help."

"Mine?"

"I kinda hoped you'd agree to work alongside me, you've got the makings of a wonderful nurse."

Aven grinned. "I can think of nothing better."

"And we can do our rounds in a sleigh."

"I'd like that."

THE END

Next book in the Series

A Sleigh Ride for Grace
By Linda Carroll-Bradd

Synopsis:
Grace Darton believes family is more important than anything...even an attentive beau. Three years ago, she broke off a courtship to tend her ailing aunt and assume management of her boardinghouse. Although her life might lack romance, she and her younger sister, Kerrie, strive to provide a family atmosphere for their boarders. But is it really enough?

Darach MacLean thought he had his future planned—he and his love, Grace, were to marry and move to Golden City for him to attend the Colorado School of Mines. But she stayed behind. As a new graduate, he returns to Spur Springs to either win her back or purge her from his life forever. His sweet Grace has become a successful businesswoman and is being wooed by the mayor. Can Darach find the way back into her heart or has he returned too late?

Link:
https://www.amazon.com/gp/product/B0D34RFGGM

About the Author

Jo Dawson grew up on a dairy farm in Wellsford, a small town in the North Island of New Zealand. She spent fifteen years as a teacher in New Zealand and abroad, before becoming a stay-at-home mum and completing her graduate degree in Theology.

She has lived in Australia and the USA for a time, and these experiences have added to her love of people and history. Blessed with a vivid imagination and the love of classical literature and historical fiction, Jo virtually grew up best friends with Anne Shirley, romping with Jo March and her sisters, sailing a raft down the Mississippi with Huckleberry Finn or living in the 'little house' with Laura Ingalls.

Born and raised in a strong Christian family, Jo's faith is at the centre of who she is, with a lifetime of being involved in churches and Christian camps. These two loves, literature and the Lord, have inevitably converged into writing compelling stories of strong Christian women, courageously facing the hardships of life on the frontier. It is her hope that women of all ages would find encouragement from her heroines' experiences that, while fiction, so often mirror even our modern lives.

Jo currently resides in the small North Island town of Waipu in New Zealand, where she lives with her husband, and a very lazy cat.

Other books by J. L. Dawson

Journeys of the Heart Series
Awakening of the Heart
Shepherd of the Heart
Decisions of the Heart
A Home for the Heart
Blessings of the Heart
Legacies of the Heart

Douglas Falls Series
Prequel: The Cost of Duty
A Duty to Love
Twixt Duty and Love
A Duty to Family
The Duty of a Father
A duty to serve.

Multiple Author Series (Standalone books).

Hers to Redeem Book 14: Aaron's Anguish
Hers to Redeem Book 18: Mitchell's Misfortune
Hers to Redeem Book 21: Robbie's Roaming
Hers to Redeem Book 22: Rueben's Risk
Winning His Devotion, Book 8: Ezra's Duty
Second Chance Groom Book 9: Romancing the Attorney
Double Trouble Book 10: Jacob's Brides
Double Trouble Book 14: Andy' Brides
A Sleigh Ride For Aven.

Standalone Books

To Love Nate – A Companion to Aaron's Anguish.

Where to find these books:
https://www.amazon.com/stores/J-L-Dawson/author
www.jodawsonauthor.com to sign up for my newsletter
jldawsonauthor@yahoo.com to write to the author
Jo Dawson and **J. L. Dawson Author**
-on Instagram and Facebook

Made in the USA
Columbia, SC
27 September 2024

42536156R00114